It nearly killed him, but he got out of the bed, holding on to the bedpost and his breath.

Dane's chest felt like someone had used him for a punching bag. As for his head…he reached up, felt the bandage there. He pulled the sheet with him, wrapping it awkwardly around his waist. He had to get out of there. He had to find his clothes….

He made it to the window on legs that felt like water, pushed the curtains aside and grabbed on to the window frame for support. Outside, a winter world greeted him, winter, not summer. *It was June.* How could there be snow?

He knew this farm. He'd been here before. He was back where it all started, last December, when his entire life had been destroyed in one fell swoop.

And the woman who said she was Calla Jones, had shown him Calla Jones's identification…

Winter not summer.

Something bone-deep and dark rushed him and he felt his knees shaking, hard.

Dear Reader,

What's not to love about a snowbound story? Throw in a supernatural time shift, a secret identity, a swirling mystery and a killer waiting to strike and you know you're in Haven—where anything can happen, and probably will, since the earthquake that triggered a wave of paranormal activity rippling across the tiny town.

In *A Hero's Redemption* Christmas-tree grower Calla Jones has enough on her hands with a blizzard bearing down when she discovers a barely conscious stranger on the road outside her farm. A stranger who can't tell her his name. Her questions grow as she finds signs that his wrists were recently bound. Then the stranger tells her he knows she is in danger, but can't tell her why.... Dane McGuire knows he's been to Haven Christmas Tree Farm before—when he was framed for murder. Now he has a chance to rewrite the past, but only if he can find the truth in time to save Calla's life.

Romantic, emotional, chilling and otherworldly...
Welcome back to Haven, West Virginia.

Love,

Suzanne McMinn

Suzanne McMinn

A HERO'S REDEMPTION

Romantic
SUSPENSE

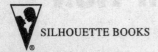

SILHOUETTE BOOKS

ISBN-13: 978-0-373-27555-7
ISBN-10:   0-373-27555-2

A HERO'S REDEMPTION

Visit Silhouette Books at www.eHarlequin.com

Printed in U.S.A.

Books by Suzanne McMinn

Silhouette Romantic Suspense

Her Man To Remember #1324
Cole Dempsey's Back in Town #1360
*The Beast Within #1377
*Third Sight #1392
*Deep Blue #1405
**Secrets Rising #1474
**A Hero's Redemption #1485

*PAX
**Haven

SUZANNE McMINN

is an award-winning author of two dozen novels, including contemporary paranormal romance, romantic suspense and contemporary romantic comedy, as well as a medieval trilogy. She lives on a farm in the mountains of West Virginia where she is plotting her next book and enjoying the simple life with her family, friends and many, many cats. Check out her upcoming books and blog at www.suzannemcminn.com.

With love to 52.

Prologue

Haven, West Virginia

Lightning cracked, flaring into the dark vehicle, the heavy June night outside suddenly pressing down on the prison transport van, reaching inside, tightening the air. Still dressed in the suit he'd worn to the sentencing, Dane McGuire forgot that his wrists were bound by handcuffs linked to a metal restraining belt at his waist and tried to reach up, touch his face, feel the strange humming pressure filling his head.

In the matter of the State vs. Dane McGuire in the murder of Calla Jones, the jury finds the defendant, Dane McGuire, guilty.

The prison transport van took a sharp mountain turn in the night, bouncing Dane—the sole occupant in the back—against the side of the vehicle. The chain connecting the shackles at his ankles rattled in the dark of the rear holding cage.

Guilty, guilty, guilty.

If only he hadn't gone to Calla Jones's farm. If only he'd arrived a few hours earlier, or later, or—

Lightning shot down again, and the humming turned into a stinging in his skin, all over. The van jerked from side to side and he hit the hard wall of the vehicle as he was thrown, first to one side, then the other. For a split second, he thought he was okay, he was in one piece, maybe just a pothole, then the back end of the van came up, tossing him like a ball, and the vehicle plowed end over end. Time suspended in some awful slow motion, turning, just turning, his body flying out of the seat belt. The last thing he knew was impact and his head striking something hard.

He opened his eyes to darkness, blinking in agonized waves of nausea. Cold. He was so cold. Freezing cold. He battled to move by instinct, to lift himself up, every motion dazed, painful.

The mountain road stretched out before him, empty but for a shimmering wave of some thick vapor that disappeared before his eyes, rushing away in an eerie whoosh that left nothing but silence. Dane's heartbeat filled the void, heavy, stumbling.

The van, the guards—

There was nothing but eerie stillness. Stillness and…something soft and frozen falling on his face. He looked down, confused, seeing the snowy ditch where he'd fallen, seeing the shackles on his wrists and ankles…gone.

He felt himself fall back, hit the ditch again, and he wondered if he was already dead.

Chapter 1

She'd never touched a dead body before and she didn't want to start now.

Chuck was practically beside himself, the yellow Lab dancing back and forth, barking madly. Do something, he was telling her. Look what I found for you. She jerked into action, half ran, half slid into the ditch, instinct overcoming shock. Ice blew sideways, stinging her cheeks.

She dropped to her knees where the stranger lay, still, utterly still. He wore dark slacks and a white button-down shirt and tie, no suit jacket or overcoat, ridiculous for this weather, and she forced herself to reach out, turn him over. Oh God. That was blood at the dark hairline of his temple. Frozen blood.

His lips were almost white in the scant light of the early storm-dark. The West Virginia mountains were in for the blizzard of all blizzards if forecasters were right, and she didn't doubt it, not after the way temps had dropped sharply from noon on. She hoped she wouldn't have to cancel the "choose-and-cut" for this weekend, the last for this year's Haven Christmas Tree Farm season. She needed a good season, and the weather wasn't helping. It hadn't been a good year altogether, starting with an earthquake last spring that had damaged her house and barn, costing her some serious money in repairs. Now she'd lost both her employees in the peak of her season and if that wasn't enough, her past was rearing its ugly head again. Now this.

A sick lump filled her throat. She tore off a glove, pushed back her hood, reached for the man's neck to find an artery, laid her cheek over his face—was he breathing? She couldn't feel a pulse, but her fingers were almost instantly numb. Wind blew. God, she couldn't tell.

Chuck barked again, running circles around the man's body. She lifted her head. Icy pellets pecked her face. No, that was snow now. And it was thickening quickly, a world of white suddenly spinning around her. She shivered even inside her thick parka, turning her gaze back to the man. There was ice on his lips, on his eyebrows, his hair. And that blood, frozen on his brow. What had happened to him? Had he fallen, or been attacked? And how the hell had he ended up here? It was miles down the mountain to town.

The man's eyes opened and she screamed. Screamed and fell back, on her ass, hard. Chuck went nuts, barking and jumping.

"Oh, my God. Oh, my God." She scrambled back to the man's side. "You're alive." *He was alive.* Her heart slammed into her throat and it was all she could think for a full second, then— "Are you okay?" No, dammit, stupid question. He was so not okay, that was obvious. Who the hell was he and how had he gotten here were better questions, and suddenly she was scared of him. He was a stranger, a bloody stranger in a ditch on the side of the road in front of her property.

No. His mouth formed the word but he couldn't get it out, or she couldn't hear it over the hammering of her own pulse. No, he wasn't okay, he was telling her, and God, he was gray, frozen. She couldn't leave him here. She'd never turned her back on anything or anyone hurt, but—

"Can you get up? Can you walk?"

His eyes held her, glassy, bright in his ashen face. Blue, she thought, but she couldn't be sure and the light was going fast. He just kept staring at her, and she couldn't have looked away if she'd tried. He didn't try to say anything else. He had to be hypothermic, and he was hurt— And there was no place to take him but the house, where she lived alone, except for Chuck. Alone, just how she liked it.

And now— She'd call for help. Maybe someone could still get up the mountain.

Maybe.

She was lying to herself. She'd be lucky if the phones even worked now, and she knew damn well the roads from Haven would be impassable at this point. In the rural mountains outside Haven, cell phone coverage was nonexistent.

"Come on," she shouted, the wind whipping at her words. She wasn't sure he could hear her, or understand her. She reached for his shoulders, pulling him to a sitting position. He felt heavy, muscular, but utterly helpless, and that should have made her feel better. He was weak—what could he do to her? Nothing. But his condition just scared her more.

He could still die.

She grabbed his arm now. "Help me, dammit!"

she yelled at him. Something inside him seemed to snap to understanding. He made it to his feet then instantly buckled at the knees. If he lost consciousness again— She grabbed him around the waist, holding him up. "You've got to walk. Please! I can't do this alone!"

If he was an inch, he was six feet tall. She was five-seven herself, but not near his weight, and just getting him out of the ditch almost did her in. He slipped, twice, and it was all she could do to keep them moving forward then up the winding driveway, Chuck barking and bouncing alongside.

The lights from the front windows of her house came into view as they rounded the curve, and she could have collapsed with relief. Nearly there. She'd left her other glove behind in the ditch and her hand was nearly frozen from the exposure. She couldn't even imagine how much colder he must be. He felt like a block of ice in her arms, a very solid, very tall block of ice.

One foot in front of the other. The front porch looked like a mountain all by itself. She could feel him struggling as he made the first step, and she was scared to death he was going to tumble backward and take her with him.

When they reached the door she let go of him with one hand to grab the knob, push it open. He weaved on his feet as if he was going to fall over right there and she threw her arm back around him.

"No! Not here!" She had to get him warmed up, and there was no time to lose.

In the light of the small front room, the man's gaze connected, glassy and lost, but he kept his feet as if by sheer force of will. She kicked the door shut behind Chuck, who made a beeline for the kitchen and his food bowl. The first bedroom was hers and she didn't think twice. She'd pretty much turned the second bedroom into an office, the bed in there piled with boxes of soaping supplies for her side business. He was far too tall for the short couch in her front room.

She maneuvered him around a small table, between an overstuffed chair and the couch, into the small hallway. Her room was dark, but there was enough light from the front room to see the bed.

A groan escaped him as he literally fell onto the bed. She reached for the lamp on the night table, then the phone.

Please, please, please—

"Dammit." She slammed the phone down, useless as she'd known it would be, and looked back at the stranger in her house. The enormity of it all hit her.

There was a stranger in her bed, and if she didn't do something, the right something, he could die. In her bed. Her knees were shaking, and not from the cold.

He was ashen, but even so, she realized with a shock that he was handsome, his jaw square, his cheeks planed, his nose straight, his hair dark, clipped short. He was maybe in his mid-thirties. He looked half-dead now, but he appeared to be fit and athletic in general, broad-shouldered and lean. Blood matted his temple and her pulse stumbled as she realized she wasn't the only one shaking.

Get his core temperature up then she'd clean his wound, figure out what to do next. And she was going to have to get his clothes off. They were icy, and when they thawed, they'd be wet.

He looked so disoriented, she didn't think he was going to be a lot of help.

Her head reeled just a little. She couldn't remember the last time she'd touched a man, let alone a naked man, and that he was helpless as a kitten didn't make her feel better. Panic didn't have to be rational, and neither did marrow-deep fears.

She tore off her parka, dropped it on the floor and approached the bed, sitting down gingerly on the edge of it. He looked huge, filling up her bed.

She reached for his hand. God, it was so cold. She pressed it between both of hers, rubbing in what warmth she could. "Hey." To whatever extent he could help, cooperate, she'd need it.

His eyes opened, blinked. Blue. They really were blue. Searing blue. Her stomach jumped.

She let go of his hand, the awkwardness and strange intimacy rearing that ugly, irrational panic again. She spoke quickly.

"I can't get help right now. The phone's out. I need you to stay awake if you can. I need to get you out of these wet clothes." She reached for his tie, unknotted it. It was a safe place to start. "Maybe tomorrow morning the phones will be working, or I can drive you down the mountain." In truth, either possibility was slim, but she kept talking, hoping it would give him something to focus on, keep him awake. "I hope there isn't someone worrying about you tonight."

She received nothing other than a blank look in response.

Surely he had a family, maybe even a wife. He was clean-cut, good-looking, nice clothes. Without thinking, her gaze fell to his hands. No ring.

"Are you from Haven?" she asked. She pulled and the tie slid out from around his neck without him having to move.

"Haven?"

His voice was slurred, a little raspy. Familiar in a way she couldn't quite place.

"Haven. You know where you are, right? You're in Haven, West Virginia. Actually we're a little outside Haven here. This is Haven Christmas Tree Farm."

He was watching her with that startlingly lost look again. She reached for the buttons on his shirt and suddenly, sharply, he moved one hand and gripped hers. Stared, just stared at her with such intensity she felt her pulse bang.

She swallowed hard. "Come on. You've got to get out of these clothes," she said, trying to pull her hand away. In an effort to distract him, she asked him another question. "How did you get here?"

"Accident. I—" He squeezed his eyes shut as if he were in pain.

"Accident where? I didn't see a car."

He still hadn't let go of her hand and his cold grip was shockingly strong.

"Come on," she said again.

His blue gaze blinked and she finally extricated her hand. She moved off the bed, needing that bit of distance. She yanked at the electric blanket cord that was tangled underneath it, hit the highest setting then got back to the bed, to him. She took the buttons of his shirt from the top down, quickly.

Outside, wind howled and the windows were completely dark now. The phones were already out—how much longer before she lost electricity? She had a generator, but it was dicey at best, old and in need of replacement.

She was midway down his shirt when he reached for the buttons as if trying to help, but she could see right away that his frozen fingers weren't going to cooperate on such a detailed task. She finished the job for him then slipped her arm around him.

He felt hard, solid and so heavy. He managed to lean up for a second, just long enough for her to pull the shirt off one arm then he sank back with a groan, closing his eyes again.

She gently tugged the shirt out from under his back. His chest and shoulders, naked in the spill of golden lamplight, were broad and muscular and she realized she was staring at him. She pulled the sleeve down and off the other arm and saw the marks on his wrists.

Sometime, very recently, he'd been bound.

"Oh, my God," the woman cried softly. "What happened to you?"

Everything hurt, especially opening his eyes. Dane McGuire's vision swam, but slowly, in increments, he tried once again to focus on the woman leaning over him. She lifted his hand, touching his wrist. There were bruised marks circling it.

"What happened to you?" she repeated.

Her hair was thick, like a dark cloud, falling around her slender face. Light from the lamp behind her framed her like a halo of fire.

He could hear wind moaning, the creaking of the house in the storm.

That's why he was so cold. He'd been out there, in the storm. She'd brought him up to the house, gotten him inside. She'd saved his life.

He'd been in an accident. He remembered slashing pain, the force as his body made impact, then— Her. He remembered her…

"Who…?" he whispered roughly. His tongue felt thick, unfamiliar even as his still-swimming vision registered recognition. He remembered *her*.

"Calla," she said.

Jones. Calla Jones.

"Jones," she finished

His mind reeled. It wasn't possible. She couldn't be Calla Jones.

"Can you tell me yours?" she asked.

He stared at her for a beat that seemed to last forever. Pain streaked through his temples and he drew a sharp breath. The pain from his bruised ribs almost had him blacking out.

"Don't try to talk anymore," she said sharply. He felt her fingers brush the skin at his waistband. "I'm sorry. I shouldn't have tried to ask you anything, not now."

He struggled to stay conscious, to focus on her, this woman who couldn't be real, couldn't be who she said she was. She was a dream, a fantasy. Her eyes were brown, the softest shade of brown he'd ever seen. And she was pretty. So pretty.

She was pretty and she was taking his pants off.

His clothes were wet. That was it. She was just trying to make him warm. He tried to help again, reached for the button of the pants. His stiff fingers shook and wouldn't bend right. He felt her warm fingers brushing his away. Her long cloud-hair swished across his cold, bare stomach as she leaned over him, then slid away as she moved down the bed, pulled on his shoes.

He felt like a baby. He forced himself up and black spots popped across his vision.

"Just let me do it," she entreated. He heard her soft voice from far away, but he could feel her right there, her soothing touch as she pulled off his clothes. Then she was back. "Come on, you have to get under the covers." She reached for him, rolled him to the side, then back as she moved the covers, tucked them around him now.

He'd never been so cold in his life—bone-deep cold even as he could feel the heat of the electric blanket against his skin. For a dream, this one was awfully painful. Inside, deep inside, he was freezing. He drifted, his eyes too heavy... She came and went and he was barely aware of her, then he felt her hands, gently, at his temples and something stinging—

Pure pain ricocheted through his head and his eyes burst open. He moved and more agony seared his chest.

"God, don't move. I think your ribs are bruised or broken. I don't know. I'm trying to be careful, but this is a bad cut."

He fell back, sucking painful air into his lungs. His limbs felt like jelly. He didn't think he could move again if his life depended on it. It hurt too much.

"Just be still," she said sternly and he focused on the seductive sound of her voice. He heard something tear, felt her fingers taping something to his head. Felt himself floating, and he went willingly.

This dream might hurt, but reality wasn't any better. In reality, Calla Jones was dead.

Chapter 2

He woke, disoriented. He couldn't see anything. He was blind. Then the lamp beside the bed popped on. He blinked, light hurting his eyes.

The windows were dark. Everything was still, silent.

His vision cleared slowly. Faded wallpaper covered the upper half of the room, white wainscoting at the bottom. A quilt in a ringed pattern hung on the opposite wall between an antique dresser and a chair.

A wave of panic washed over him. He pushed up from the bed, hissing in agony as he swung his

legs to the floor. Gripping the corner of the head-
board, he straightened on wavering knees.

He was naked. The woman— There had been
a woman. He'd thought she'd said her name was
Calla Jones, even thought she'd looked like Calla
Jones. But that wasn't possible. He'd heard her
wrong, imagined the resemblance.

She'd taken his clothes off, everything but his
briefs, warmed him in her bed. And he was sure
it was *her* bed. Everything surrounding him in the
room—the pretty perfume and cream bottles
marching across the old dresser, the flowered
wreath on the wall, the lacy coverlet on the bed—
screamed feminine occupation.

He hung on to the knobbed corner of the head-
board again while he took shallow, agonizing
breaths and willed himself to stay upright even as
black pain threatened to consume him. He tried to
focus, assess the damage—his head throbbed, his
ribs screamed. But everything worked, if pain-
fully. He wasn't broken, just bruised.

And he was in trouble. Terrible trouble. He had
to get dressed. *He had to get out of here.*

"Oh, my God." He heard a rush of footsteps
through the agony wrapping his mind. "Get back
in bed. What are you doing? If you pass out and
fall, you'll just hurt yourself more!"

Arms slipped around his waist; soft, caring arms, guiding him back down. Relief buckled his knees and he didn't fight her, let her ease him back onto the bed in one miserable, slow move.

"You have to rest. You can't do this." The woman's voice was clipped, frustrated. Warm brown eyes sparked at him. Warm brown eyes that looked just like Calla Jones's eyes. The resemblance was startling.

But it was just that, a resemblance. Calla Jones was dead.

She tucked blankets back around him. "I think you've got some bruised ribs, but I'm not a doctor. And you are not a very good patient."

She chewed her lip in the way he remembered, suddenly, she had before. She was looking at him, too, and the very real, very fragile awareness in her gaze almost hurt to see.

"We lost electricity. I had to go outside and get the generator going," she said.

That explained the pitch-black he'd woken to, and the lamp suddenly popping on. But it didn't explain *her*. She started to rise and without thinking, he reached for her hand, stopping her.

"Don't go." His mouth was so dry, he could barely get the words out. "Who are you?"

She stared at him. "I'm just going to put your

clothes in the laundry." She tugged her hand from his, impatient, yet there was something more than impatience in her eyes. Something wounded. "My name is Calla. Calla Jones. This is Haven Christmas Tree Farm."

His head reeled, and for a moment he couldn't focus or think. Then her face cleared in his vision, Calla Jones's face, and he saw her eyes gaze to his wrists.

"It looks," she whispered, "as if you'd been bound. What happened to you?"

Of course his wrists had been bound. His ankles had been shackled, too. And all of that meant that Calla Jones was long dead. He was dreaming, had to be dreaming. What other explanation was there?

"I don't know what's happened to me," he said, his voice hoarse suddenly. He'd lost his mind, maybe. *I was being transported, bound, to prison for your murder.* Dane supposed he could tell her that.

She was looking at him, confusion in her gaze. She seemed young, he thought suddenly, really young, with slender hollows in her cheeks and those soft, soft brown eyes, even as he could detect the faint lines around her eyes that proved she wasn't really that young at all. She was thirty-one. The district attorney had said so. The D.A.

had passed around all sorts of photographs of her bloodied body to the jury, posted enlarged shots on huge easel boards, shoved them in front of his face while he sat in the witness box.

"You can't be Calla Jones," he rasped desperately, almost angrily, suddenly. What game was this? If it wasn't a dream, then could it be some kind of cruel hoax? Anything was possible. After all, someone had set him up for murder. Now what?

He could hear a huff of exasperation, then she got up from the bed, marched to the dresser, grabbed something—her purse, he realized, and pulled a wallet from inside. She flipped the small leather case open and held it up in front of him.

"Look."

Calla Jones's name leaped up at him from the West Virginia driver's license.

His vision spun to a tiny pinprick of light and blood and her. Slicing pain ripped through his head. No. Calla Jones had died six months ago. No one knew that better than him. He'd been on his way to prison for the crime, a crime he hadn't committed, but that had stopped mattering a long time ago. His life as he'd known it had been over. He'd almost accepted it. One minute, he'd been an attorney for Ledger Pharmaceuticals. The next, he was a number headed for prison. Almost, but not quite. He'd never accept it, not really.

"Tell me the truth," he gasped hoarsely, reaching frantically for her hand again. "You're with them, aren't you?"

"Them? Who are you talking about?"

"The ones who did this to me."

"The ones who did what?" she whispered, and his vision reeled backward as if sucked through a vortex, and he could see her, now, backing away, her hand slipping from his. He was scaring her.

But she was scaring him and the spinning of his vision was making him sick.

"The ones who did this to you," he said, almost blindly, the edges of his vision folding together now, darkness closing in.

"Did what to me?" Panic rose sharp in her voice. "I don't know what you're talking about!"

"The ones who killed you."

Then the black swallowed him whole.

The hair lifted at Calla's nape. She felt cold again suddenly, and more than a little unnerved.

The stranger had passed out now. He'd been half out of it even when he'd had his eyes open. *The ones who killed you.*

Was he crazy? Or just disoriented? Maybe he

didn't know what he was saying. He hadn't been able to tell her his name. Did he even remember his name? He had a head injury.

And he was freaking her out.

She picked up his wet clothes and walked out into the front room. The urge to check the locks on the door was suddenly almost unbearable, as if she thought someone was out there, poised to break in. The stranger's words reverberated in her head. She shook herself. It was snowing so hard, she'd barely been able to see when she'd gone out to the shed to turn on the generator. She'd been almost frightened she wouldn't be able to get back to the house. Thank God she hadn't had to go that far.

There was no one lurking outside waiting to kill her, not in this storm, and not ever. There was someone *inside*, and that was enough to make her uncomfortable. He couldn't hurt her, not in his condition, she repeated to herself. And she wasn't that twenty-year-old girl she'd been once, either. She wouldn't let anyone hurt her, not ever again. The old panic deep in her gut didn't believe her sometimes, but she did, in her heart, in her head. She was older, wiser, tougher. And the stranger was just out of his mind from hypothermia and possibly concussed.

Chuck was stretched out in the middle of the floor, flat on his back, legs splayed out in total abandon.

"This is all your fault," she said softly as she passed the dog. His tail thumped the floor lightly but he didn't get up. He was exhausted from his big day of following her around the farm, chasing the new kittens, and finding a stranger in the ditch for her.

Not that Calla could regret finding the man, John Doe for now, tonight, since she didn't know his name. If she hadn't found him, he'd have died. And she couldn't bear that thought, knowing that bringing him in meant she'd saved a life. And it hadn't really been Chuck's fault, though he was the one who'd directed her to the ditch.

How had he come to be here? There were only two reasons she would have expected people at Haven Christmas Tree Farm today—to get a tree or to talk to her about a job, and in this weather, she hadn't expected either, though there was always room for a miracle after losing both her farmhands this week. Pete had done another of his disappearing acts then Jimmy had taken off the next day. Something had scared the bejeebers out of him in the woods. Probably a bear. But there'd been no talking sense to Jimmy, especially with the recent nonsense going around town.

It had all started after a so-called paranormal detective with some cable TV channel had reported earthquakes could release "positive ions" into the atmosphere and trigger supernatural activity. She was pretty sure everything since was the product of the town's collective overactive imagination. Either that or it was the mayor's latest attempt at beefing up tourism. She just hoped it meant more people came to Haven to buy Christmas trees.

She flipped the light on in the small utility room off the kitchen and dumped the bundle of clothes on the butcher block counter beside the washer. The shirt was soiled from where he'd lain on the ground and she set it aside. She'd try some stain treatment, but it might be hopeless. She stuck her hands in the pockets of the pants, hoping for something, some identification, some clue to the stranger.

Nothing. No wallet—she'd noticed that as soon as she'd stripped his clothes off, but she'd been hoping— She started to pull her hand out then realized there *was* something. Small and wet.

She pulled out the folded bit of paper, carefully laid it on the counter and used her fingernail to slowly pull the soggy pieces apart to reveal the printed logo at the top. It was a receipt. A-Plus

Cleaners, Haven, WV. There was a hand-scrawled drop-off date. June 7, she thought, but the date was blurred, the ink smeared from moisture. It looked like June 7…of next year? She picked up the wet receipt, too quickly, to hold it up to the bare bulb above the counter and it tore in her hands. She put the two halves back down on the counter, and there was that chill lifting the hair at the back of her neck again. Jeez, what was wrong with her?

Of course the date wasn't next June. It had to be last June. The stranger must not wear his suits very often for the receipt to still be in his pocket in December. But it didn't matter and she couldn't read it now anyway. The receipt had torn right across the year. And she was just still good and freaked out about his earlier comment and that whole positive ions hooey. She focused on what the receipt could mean.

The stranger hadn't seemed to recognize the name Haven when she'd asked him if he was from here, but clearly he'd had tailoring done on his clothes in town. Calla had never seen him around, but that didn't mean much. She didn't know everyone in Haven even though she'd grown up there. She'd been gone for nearly twelve years between college, graduate school and the career she'd thought would be her lifetime work. Then it had all gone very, very wrong, and she'd come home to lick her wounds, start over. Haven hadn't changed much, though it had certainly grown in population.

Once the phones were back, if the stranger still didn't remember his name, she'd be able to give the receipt to the authorities. They could call the shop. Maybe they'd have records, be able to track down his ID. Or maybe his confusion tonight was temporary. He'd know his name tomorrow.

Not that that was her problem. Once the roads were clear, he would be someone else's problem. All she had to do was make sure he lived till then. And if he would just stay in bed, he would probably be fine. His skin had already begun to feel warmer to the touch, and his color had been coming back.

She popped the pants in the dryer and set the stained shirt to soak. And she wondered if she would really forget the stranger as easily as that, as easily as dropping him off at the county hospital or the police station, depending on his condition when she could get him out of here. She checked on the stranger again. He was alive, sleeping. She went to the living room, grabbed the folded quilt off the back of it and stretched out. She tried really hard not to think about the fact that a man was sleeping in the next room. In her bed. A stranger.

Mostly, she tried not to think about the morning.

Chapter 3

Dawn crept through lace at the windows and Dane McGuire stared at the rectangle of light in the shadowed room, his head throbbing, his mind searching through some disembodied sea of broken pieces that slipped and slid on waves of pain. The courthouse, the conviction, the crash— The woman who couldn't be Calla Jones.

It nearly killed him but he got out of the bed, holding on to the bedpost and his breath. His chest felt like someone had used him for a punching bag. As for his head— He reached up, felt the bandage there. He pulled the sheet with him,

wrapping it awkwardly around his waist. He had
to get out of here. He had to find his clothes. She'd
said something about putting them in the laundry.

He made it to the window on legs that felt like
water, pushed the curtains aside and grabbed on
to the window frame for support. Outside, a winter
world greeted him, winter, not summer. *It was
June*. How could there be snow? The sun broke
through the clouded morning, and he blinked
against the suddenly bright light on all that white
landscape. *Snow*. There was a barn, snow drifting
high against it, right where he knew it would be.
The greenhouse and the trees, the mountains
scraping sky above. And the snow was still falling,
light now, but continuous. He knew this farm.
He'd been here before. This really *was* Haven
Christmas Tree Farm. He was back where it all
started, last December, when his entire life had
been destroyed in one fell swoop.

And the woman who said she was Calla Jones,
looked like Calla Jones, had shown him Calla
Jones's identification— He pivoted, ignoring the
rush of pain and wave of sickness. The dresser
where the woman had gotten the purse with the
driver's license was there. There were photographs all lined up; a little girl, a teenager, an
adult, a woman as she grew. A lifetime in a few

pictures. There was a framed West Virginia University diploma with Calla Jones's name. A stack of envelopes, bills, addressed to Calla Jones.

Winter, not summer.

A calendar was tacked to the wall with a stick pin, open to December of the previous year. There was a CD player on the dresser. He fumbled for it, pushed the button. Classic rock poured out. He pushed it off the CD mode, switched to radio. No cord, so it was on battery. Fuzz. He pushed the selector until he found a clear station. More music. Another one with a commercial jingle. He kept pushing the button. *Weather for today, December 20, in the Appalachian foothill region—*

Something bone-deep and dark rushed him and he felt his knees shaking, hard.

Calla woke with a start, her eyes blinking open against the pale dawn shafting through the windows of the front room, nerves strung taut— A bang. That's what had woken her. A loud bang from the back of the house—

She jerked forward, tossing the blanket, uncurling her legs, remembered the stranger and— She rushed to the next room.

The radio played the day's news to an empty bed. He was gone.

Her blood pumped hot in the chilly room. Panic at the stranger's disappearance combined with the realization that there was no heat. The generator must have died.

And the stranger, the stranger who was in no fit state to travel on foot, was gone. He'd die out there.

The forecast airing on the radio was for a bad one, the storm expected to last at least another day, steady snow this morning and increasing again by noon to blizzard-strength. Mountainous roads were already impassable. People were being warned to stay home, even in the towns. Electric and phone service out for thousands of homes. The governor was calling for a state of emergency, requesting federal assistance in clearing roads and restoring basic services.

She rushed out of the room. The sound had come from the back of the house. Grabbing and shoving on shoes, she ran, through the kitchen, through the utility room, blasting out into the icy morning. As she took the first step, she slipped and then slid on the concrete stair. She grappled for the railing, desperate to keep from landing on her ass. Failed. The heels of her bare hands hit the snow-covered steps, barely breaking her fall. The cold impact stunned her for a beat then arms swept her, warm arms in the cold snow.

Blinking, her vision clearing, she saw it was him.

"Get in the house!" Calla barked at him, angry, she realized. Very angry. It was his fault she was out here. Saving his life yet again and mad about that, too. She didn't want to have to save his life, didn't want to have anything to do with him.

He stared back at her, snow on his very long, very dark eyelashes that she noticed suddenly, sharply. He didn't say anything, just pulled her to her feet, set her steady and stepped back. He wasn't even wearing a shirt, she realized.

"Are you crazy?" she yelled at him. He was wearing only the pants she'd dried last night, and his shoes. His stained shirt was still soaking, she remembered. Then she saw him wincing in pain. His ribs, she remembered that, too. He'd hurt his ribs. And maybe he *was* crazy.

But he'd die out here.

"Just get back in the house," she said, lowering her voice, though the words still came out clipped. And shaking. Her teeth were starting to chatter. "You'll freeze out here. And if you want to kill yourself, that's fine, but not on my watch."

She wanted to tell him he deserved to freeze, but that wasn't true or necessary or kind. It would just be venting. Maybe he *did* have a head injury.

He was still staring back at her through the snow as if in some kind of shock, though he'd been with it enough to come to her aid. What the hell had driven him out into the snow half-dressed?

He didn't move so she grabbed his arm with one hand, the railing with the other, and dragged him back the few steps to the door, pushed him inside ahead of her. She shoved the door shut with a slam. She was back in her house with a frozen, mysterious stranger.

She stood there, shivering.

"You're underdressed," she said into the sharp quiet of the house. She crossed the utility room, grabbing open the cellar door.

The utility room was an add-on to the old building, connecting what used to be a separate cellar to the main house. There were boxes and boxes stacked against one wall of her grandfather's things and a hanging rack with some of his old clothes. She jerked open a box and grabbed the first shirt on top, a heavy plaid flannel shirt. Another box held folded jeans. She pulled down a jacket from the rack.

"Here," she said, returning to the stranger. "Put this on." She handed him the shirt and the jeans, which would be heavier protection than the slacks he'd come with last night. Then she set the jacket on top of the big chest freezer across from the washer and dryer. "And if you take a hankering to go strolling outside again, wear a jacket!"

Her irritation vanished as she watched him slide his arms awkwardly into the flannel shirt and try to use his frozen fingers to connect the buttons. She marched the few steps between them and took matters into her own hands. Her knuckles brushed his solid, very muscular chest. Something she would have been better off avoiding. She was actually turned on. It was ludicrous. Here he was, a stranger, half out of his head for all she knew, and she couldn't stop noticing that he was extremely attractive.

She finished with the buttons. She felt his eyes following her every nervous movement and she blamed the cold that her own hands were shaking, almost as useless as his.

"Come on," she said abruptly, stepping back from him. He was still watching her. Just watching her. Like she was some unknown specimen. Well, she felt the same about him, so she supposed that was fair. "I'll fix some coffee. You need to get something warm inside you. There's a bathroom there—" She pointed it out on the way to the kitchen. "You can change your pants in there."

She headed for the kitchen, wondering if he'd come after her or go back outside. If he kept acting crazy, she'd have to let him go. She couldn't call for help at this point, and what else could she do? Tie him up? If he wanted to leave, he was free to go. She'd done everything she could.

Acting as if she didn't care when, for some stupid reason, she did, she flipped on the light over the deep farmhouse sink and set about filling the coffeemaker with water and grounds. The water was still running, but for how long?

Tension tightened her shoulders. The enormity of this storm was hitting her.

"Can I help?"

Calla felt him behind her and turned, found him standing there, in her kitchen, still watching her with those curiously daunting eyes. He was pale, but under that bloodless cold, he was a strong, fit man. She knew that. There were fine etchings of pain in his expression, but determination revealed itself in the hard line of his mouth. He looked effortlessly sexy in the flannel shirt and jeans she'd given him. They fit perfectly.

His voice... It was deep and Southern. Very typically West Virginian. Maybe that was why it had sounded so familiar somehow. She knew she had never met him before.

She would have remembered him. Oh boy, would she have remembered him.

"No. I'm fine. I've got it all set." She gestured at the coffeemaker. "You should sit down. You should probably lie down." For sure, he shouldn't be out tramping in the snow. Her heart thumped when she saw him blink rapidly. "Are you going to pass out?"

"No."

Yep, *very* determined.

She closed the distance between them, pressed her hands down on his shoulders and guided him back toward the kitchen table. It was nicked, nearly as old as the house itself, surrounded by six cane-back chairs. A carved walnut baby chair sat, long-unused, in the corner. The room, like the house, was rustic, with scarred wood floors, shelves lined with beautiful, antique canning jars she used to store dry goods, a pie safe for a cabinet. Old-fashioned ceramic jars and jugs crowded the mantel of an old stone fireplace.

She'd brought in a supply of wood the day before, and laid in extra in the utility room to keep it from getting wet. The rest lay under a tarp behind the barn, but with the way the wind had been howling all night, she wondered if that had stayed dry.

"Sit down anyway," she insisted. "I've got enough problems as it is."

He cooperated, which said something.

"I'm sorry," he said. "I don't want to cause you any trouble."

Guilt pricked her. "I didn't mean that the way it came out. I can't pick you up off the floor, that's all."

His gaze was flat, direct. "You saved my life."

"Can you tell me what happened, now? What is your name?" Did he know who he was? She'd heard of amnesia, but she'd never encountered it outside the soap operas she used to watch in college. Wasn't this a soap opera scenario? Trapped in a blizzard with a stranger who couldn't remember his name.

She might have laughed but for the lump of fear in her throat. *You're with them, aren't you?* His bizarre words from the night before rang again in her mind.

The ones who killed you.

It was all too creepy. She didn't like it.

She wanted the soap opera scenario where she got stranded on a deserted island and magically had makeup and sexy clothes to wear every day. They'd feast on bananas and speared fish and drink coconut milk till the ship found them. Yeah, she liked that one better… Except for the part where she'd have to have anything to do with a man at all.

He still hadn't answered.

She hadn't turned the lantern-style fixture on over the table. The gauzy morning sun filtering through the snow outside didn't do much to illuminate the room. The single bulb from the light over the sink created shadows across his face, revealing the cut of his jawline, the straight line of his nose, the unsettling darkness of his eyes.

Suddenly she wasn't thinking how sexy he was, how some wild, bad side of her would like it if she could just spread him on a cracker and eat him up. She was thinking instead about how she wanted to run. Far. And fast.

Even before he spoke, dread thumped, almost painful, in her veins. This wasn't the fun soap opera storyline. It was the nightmarish one.

"I don't know what happened to me," he finally said. "I don't know how I got here."

Chapter 4

She looked scared. Dane didn't blame her. He was a little scared himself, and that was a little bit of an understatement.

But it was growing more and more impossible for him to ignore what appeared to be the fantastical truth. He'd gone back in time six months, to the week of Calla Jones's murder. How? Why?

Reality stung him from every direction, and yet how could *this* be reality? He'd considered, for a few blind, mind-boggling moments, running away. Just…running away. He'd gone outside, in the snow. Half-dressed. Out of his head.

He had to start thinking clearly even while the world around him had rocked completely off its foundation. There was a freaking blizzard out there, and Calla Jones in here. His choices were limited, but heading for certain death in the frozen world gone mad outside this old farmhouse wasn't the best one. He needed time. Time to make a plan.

In the meantime, he wasn't sharing his secret with Calla Jones. Or his name. Not until he'd had time to think.

He had no idea what was going on. Yet.

Neither did he have much idea how he was going to figure it out, but it all centered around Calla Jones, didn't it? That realization shot home suddenly, nearly sucking the breath out of his chest. His life had been destroyed the day he'd come out to her farm. She'd been murdered. He'd been blamed. Now he'd somehow ended up right back here on Calla Jones's farm, six months earlier, where it all started.

And if whatever *Twilight Zone* craziness was going on rotated around Calla Jones… His nape prickled and he took a sharp breath, felt the pain. His ribs were bruised, at the very least. He was shaky, and not just from his injuries.

"You… You really don't know who you are? No idea? Nothing?"

She was staring at him like she wanted to back

up, maybe scream. Her hair, auburn-streaked, he realized now in the pale light framing her, not mere brown, was tousled—she'd been sleeping on the couch when he'd left the farmhouse. She'd slept in her clothes, he guessed. She wouldn't have had time to change before she'd come tearing out after him.

The beat stretched between them. The gurgle of the coffeemaker and wind creaking against the farmhouse filled the space.

He avoided a direct response. "I was in an accident," he said, remembering now that he'd told her that last night. "I don't know what happened." That much was true.

"I didn't see anything out there. I didn't see a car or anything."

"Maybe the accident didn't happen on the road outside your farm. Maybe I was trying to walk back to town." Really, he didn't know whether that was true or not. For all he remembered, it could be.

"You need to be looked at by a doctor. I can't get you to town, and I can't call for help. The phone's dead in the farmhouse, and cell phones don't work out here. Even if I could call, I doubt anyone could get up here right now. The roads are impassable when we have this kind of storm."

Now she did back up, as if it was hitting her, again, that she was stuck with this stranger. She had to have realized that before, and yet she'd saved him last night and had rushed out again this morning after him. She was "good people," this Calla Jones he'd been convicted of murdering. Of course, he'd known that. He'd heard her friends extol her virtues at the sentencing hearing.

"I can try to walk back to town," he said. He didn't want to leave, not now, not yet. He'd been thrown back in time, back to the very scene of the crime, for a reason. There had to be a reason. Nothing made sense, but that was why he had to stay.

He had to make sense of it. As much as he'd been ready to, crazily, run away in the storm moments before, now he knew he had to stay. Calla Jones was the key.

But Calla Jones was scared. He had to gamble that, bighearted person that she was, she wasn't going to think his tromping off in the storm was a good idea.

"No, you can't do that," she said finally. "It's snowing, and it's supposed to snow harder later. It's miles into town. You're already suffering from exposure. You'd never make it."

She chewed her lip, watched him worriedly from wary eyes. "I couldn't find any identification on you," she went on. "I did find a receipt from a dry cleaner's in town."

The suit he'd worn at the sentencing, right before he'd been loaded into the transport van, had been cleaned in Haven for his court appearance. The high-priced attorney that Carter Sloane, the Ledger CEO, had hired had taken care of it. Unfortunately Edward Jeffries hadn't taken care of much else he'd needed. Like getting him off.

She watched him with those deep brown eyes of hers, eyes flecked with amber lights, scared but concerned. They were gentle and sweet eyes.

She didn't deserve to die, not any more than he deserved to go to prison for the rest of his life. His head reeled again. It was a tall order he was setting himself up to fill, saving the both of them. And he was still in shock and having a hard time accepting this strange new reality.

He propped his elbow on the table and leaned his head into his palm, a wash of disorientation hitting him.

"Are you okay? Are you going to be sick?"

She was there, kneeling at his feet. He lifted his gaze, found hers tight on his.

He swallowed hard over the lump of dread in his throat. "I'm all right." He *had* to be all right. "I just feel like I've been beaten up by fifty guys, that's all."

"My name's Calla, in case you don't remember,"

she said. "This is Haven Christmas Tree Farm. Haven, West Virginia. It's December 20."

She'd been murdered on December 22. Whatever quirk of fate had given him this second chance, it hadn't been generous with time. He had two days...

And then would it happen all over again?

Calla Jones would die and he would end up in jail? He'd come out to her farm that day, from his office in Parkersburg where Ledger Pharmaceuticals was headquartered. He'd come on routine business—an audit had uncovered a legal form misplaced from her employee records. She hadn't even worked for Ledger for some time. She'd been in the research department, but he wasn't aware of much more than that, nor had he been much interested. He'd arrived at the farm and next thing he'd known, he'd been knocked out. He'd woken to the nightmare of her dead body and the rest was documented in court records.

Her hand rested on his knee. She was so damn nice and pretty to boot. Why would anyone want to kill her?

"I don't know what to do," she said. "I don't know what I can do to help you, but you're welcome to stay here, ride out the storm."

"Thank you. You're very kind." Very kind, and perhaps too innocent. Someone had come to her farm that day and killed her, possibly they'd been lying in wait when he'd arrived, taken advantage of the opportunity to set someone else up for the crime. Not that his lawyer had had much luck with any of the conspiracy theories he'd floated. The jury had bought the prosecutor's premise that he'd had some kind of relationship with her at Ledger, putting it all down to a crime of passion despite evidence that he'd come to Haven for a specific business purpose.

There'd been absolutely no proof that he'd had any kind of affair with Calla Jones at all, no witnesses, but the district attorney had theorized that since relationships between coworkers were frowned on at Ledger, they'd kept it secret. Motive had hardly mattered, not when there was a dead body and his fingerprints all over the murder weapon. He was an outsider in a small and clannish town, accused of killing one of their own, caught seemingly red-handed. The jury had been quick enough to believe what was in front of them, evidence of motive be damned.

He'd never had a chance.

"There's not much point being anything other than kind," Calla Jones said now. Calla Jones, alive and well and two days from death. She removed her hand from his knee, straightened.

Oddly, he missed her touch, unfamiliar as it was. He hadn't been touched with such gentleness in six months. He'd barely felt human touch at all, other than prison guards shackling and unshackling him, guiding him from place to place. The judge hadn't set a bond. He'd spent six months in the county lockup waiting for trial. The murder had been too shocking. The town had been up in arms. Bail had been a hopeless dream.

"The coffee's ready," she added, and he could hear the nervous thread in her voice.

She was kind, but maybe she wasn't as naive as he'd been thinking. She was scared of him, still. He'd have to break through her wariness. He needed to get to know her, to get to know why someone would want her dead. If it had been a crime of passion, as the "overkilling" suggested, who was passionate about Calla Jones? Passionate enough to shoot her not once but five times?

A minute later, she had a steaming cup of coffee in front of him.

"Sugar? Cream?" she asked.

He shook his head. "Black's fine."

She didn't get herself a cup and sit down with him. Instead she headed toward the back of the house again, coming back with an armful of what looked like empty plastic milk jugs. He watched, sipping the coffee that injected sorely needed heat to his veins.

"Can I help?" He had no idea what she was doing, but he wasn't going to sit here and let her do all the work.

And he needed to get her talking. Somehow. She was nervous around him and he needed to make her more comfortable.

His brain was starting to work. Now he just had to control the slight blast of nearly uncontainable excitement that hit him. He had a second chance. If this was real, if he really had gone six months back in time, he had a second chance.

And everything around him, including Calla Jones, seemed very real. If this was a dream, he didn't want to wake up now.

She placed one of the jugs in the deep sink, ignoring his offer to help. "The generator's not dependable and this storm's predicted to go through the night, at least. We're on well water here, and the well needs power to run." She turned on the faucet, started filling the container. "The generator could go bad and we'll have no power. Or the pipes could freeze. Either way, we'll have no water."

Dane downed the last of the coffee and rose. "Then we'll have no heat, either. And if this is all the firewood you've got in the house—"

She flipped around. "There's more stacked in the utility room, but you're right. It's not enough."

"Where's more?"

"Out behind the barn. Under a tarp. Should be pretty dry. I hope. You're not going out there."

"Someone has to. If the snow's going to pick up later, now's the time."

Frustration etched her face. Her eyes sparked, making her even prettier. "I'm trying to get you warmed up. Going out in the cold again is not a good idea."

"Someone has to," he repeated. "I can always warm up again."

She took a step toward him as if she might physically stop him.

"I said no." She stamped her foot.

She actually stamped her foot. He guessed she wasn't even aware of doing it.

A sudden, unexpected and truly unwanted vision of various ways Calla Jones could warm him up invaded his head. A hot trail of surprising and not-experienced-for-over-six-months sexual desire nipped at his loins.

"That was really cute," he blurted out.

"What was cute?" She looked even more irritated.

"You, stamping your foot."

"I did not stamp my foot!"

"There, you did it again!"

"I did not. Okay, maybe I did." She blushed now, and that wasn't just cute, it was sexy as hell. She swiped at her hair, brushing it out of her face. "But whatever. You're not going outside."

"And you're not doing all the work here," he countered, working on grounding himself, keeping it sane. What was he doing anyway? Flirting with her? Really, his head must still be reeling.

He couldn't even pretend to himself that this was all part of his big plan to get close to her and figure out who might want to kill her. He'd just flat-out been enjoying himself for a second, and maybe he was feeling a little heady from the sensation of having a second chance here, but that was no excuse, either.

They were in deep trouble, both of them. Trouble Calla knew and understood, and trouble she didn't. Trouble even he didn't understand.

Dane stood, swaying slightly, but he was all right. Or he would be. He certainly wasn't going to get his strength back sitting on his ass drinking coffee while she did everything.

"You're so weak you can hardly stand up," she started.

"I'm fine," he promised, steadying himself. He was shaky, but he'd make it. "I want to help. And since I'm bound and determined to do it and you can't stop me, you might as well keep filling up on water. I'll put on that jacket out there. If you've got gloves and a hat, I'll take that, too."

"You could lose your way. I'll go with you."

"The generator could die anytime. You said that. We need the water, too. How long do you think it could be before the road is cleared and electricity is back on if this storm keeps up as predicted throughout the rest of today and tonight?"

"Later in the day tomorrow if we're lucky. Maybe not till the day after. Depending on what else goes wrong along with the storm. One time when I was a kid, I was spending Christmas here with my grandfather and the storm lasted a week. There were power lines down everywhere and trees across the roads."

Her gaze drifted to the kitchen window where snow continued to swirl the air, harder already. She chewed her lip.

"Then it's pretty obvious, isn't it? There's no time to waste. We need water, and we need wood. If this gets worse, soon we won't even be able to see our way out to the barn and I can haul more wood in one trip than you can. Meanwhile, you can get the water. Divide and conquer, right?"

Dane didn't wait for her answer, a fierce need to protect Calla driving him. Maybe too fierce to be explainable, even by the circumstances. He didn't want to think about what was behind the strength of that feeling.

Chapter 5

Calla watched out the back windows of the house as the stranger disappeared into the growing veil of white blotting out the landscape. What if he didn't come back?

Whatever had possessed him to go out into the snow earlier, half-dressed, he'd seemed to come to his senses, but heading out for the wood was a madness all its own despite their need for the fuel. Under normal circumstances, it would be a short trip to the barn and back. But he had a point about the wood. He could haul more back in one trip than she could and with the way the storm was hitting this morning, harder and faster than the earlier radio forecast, soon it wouldn't be safe to attempt it at all. A second trip was out of the question.

She grabbed more of the plastic jugs from the cellar she saved during the year just for this emergency purpose. What if the storm lasted a week, like it had that time when she'd been visiting her grandfather?

A week trapped, snowbound, with a stranger.

One very sexy, very mysterious stranger.

She felt very alone in the house without him, she realized. Alone and nervous. She was used to being alone, so what was up with that? She preferred alone. Her own personal nonpracticing lesbian compound. A private joke between her and a couple of her single girlfriends in town. Nonpracticing because she wasn't actually attracted to women, and lesbian for symbolizing that she wasn't taking any crap off men anymore. Her practicing heterosexual days were over.

Except for the little tingly heat when she looked at the stranger that reminded her that she was, indeed, attracted to men. He had a voice that was low, rough, gorgeously sensual, and eyes that drowned her, all knowing and deep. She'd bet he knew just how to pleasure a woman, and that he'd pleasured plenty in his time.

He was a little scary, too. That mystery thing. Danger, Will Robinson! There was excitement in the danger and mystery of him. Stupid, stupid of her to be drawn to it.

Changing out one jug for another under the faucet, she reminded herself it didn't matter how hot he was. She didn't do trust. Not anymore. Not with men.

It was basic human compassion that made her allow him to shelter in her farmhouse until the storm passed. That was all. And she was a big fat liar to herself.

When she had all the jugs filled up, she ran back to the utility room, Chuck at her heels. He was old and not exactly an early riser, but the activity had finally roused him. Anxiety dug a hole in her stomach as she peered through the frosted light. Her heart kicked, hard, when she spied the stranger coming into focus through the snow.

He was pushing the wheelbarrow. She was so crazy-relieved to see him, it was ridiculous.

"Hurry!" she cried as she tore open the door, her voice whipping away in the wind as he staggered up the steps. Chuck darted out after her.

Snow clung to his eyebrows and lashes. His lips were nearly blue. Dammit—

She grabbed gloves and a coat of her own, going after the wood, hauling pieces at a time into the utility room where it could get dry. He came back down the steps, awkwardly grappling for the split logs, too. Together, they worked without a word, too busy rushing at their task.

"I got what I could," he gasped, collapsing finally against the big chest freezer, once they had all the wood safely inside. "This'll have to get us through. The tarp you had out there blew away when I took it off. The rest of it will be covered in snow. Is covered in snow already, I'm sure."

She called for Chuck, who she'd lost track of, and the dog came bouncing out of the white day and up the steps. She slammed the door shut behind him.

The stranger swayed as if he'd topple over. She grabbed the sleeve of his jacket.

"Come on." The utility room was cold, and he was colder. She guided him toward the front room, helped him out of the jacket and gloves, grabbing the blanket she'd slept under. "You're freezing. I'll start a fire."

"No," he argued quickly. "We've got heat now. When the generator goes out, that's time enough to start using the wood." His teeth chattered, making his words shake.

He was right. She was panicking. They had to conserve energy. She could hear the comforting sound of the farmhouse's central heating system, installed twenty years ago in the old structure, kicking on to regulate the inside temperature.

Her own hands trembling still with cold despite her shorter exposure, she ran to the kitchen for the cup he'd used earlier, filled it with the hot coffee and brought it back to him.

She sat across from him in her grandfather's comfy old recliner, curling her legs under her. Watching the stranger. Chuck circled a couple times at the foot of the recliner then settled down. What now?

"You were right," she said slowly. "I couldn't have brought all that wood back, and I wouldn't have made a second trip. The snow's too hard now." A new thought hit her. "If this goes on all night and the generator goes out, maybe you'll have saved my life, too."

Something flared in the stranger's gaze, and she felt a strange prickle along her spine.

"I'd like that," he said finally. "I'd like to save your life, Calla Jones."

Determination resonated in his voice.

He could make money just letting women listen to him speak. It was like wood bark wrapped in honey, rough and melt-your-brain smooth at once. Something nipped at the edges of her mind then fell away before she could grasp it. For a second, she'd thought again there was something familiar about his voice.

But that was impossible. She'd never met him before, she was sure of that. It had to just be that sexy West Virginia accent.

"You must be hungry," she said, distracting herself. "And if we lose the generator, it'll be nice if something's cooked. I've got plenty of food, but the stove is electric, so that won't work without the generator. I have some ground beef thawed out. I was going to make some chili last night before—" Before he showed up. Then she'd forgotten all about food. "A big pot of chili. That would be good. Do you like chili?"

She was, she recognized, practically babbling. It was nuts.

It was setting in, the fact that this was no short-term thing. She was trapped with him, the stranger with no name, for the duration. Another day at least, maybe longer.

"Chili sounds just fine. Thank you."

"I don't know what to call you," she said suddenly. "I feel funny not calling you anything."

"*Hey you* works." His hard lips curved.

Oh God. He had a killer smile. Of course. She should have known. No surprise there.

He had a killer everything.

"Not very friendly," she pointed out. How friendly did she plan on being? Curl of heat, down low. Stop it, she warned herself. Besides, this was serious. He didn't know his name. How strange was that? She couldn't imagine.

"Call me whatever you want," he said. "Tom, Dick, Harry."

"John. John Doe. J.D." She liked that for some reason. John was too plain. J.D. suited.

He'd leaned his head back on the couch, closed his eyes. "Whatever you like."

"Are you okay?"

He opened his eyes to narrow slits, meeting her worried question without lifting his head. "I'm okay."

"If you die, I won't like that." She was suddenly scared. What if he had some internal injuries she didn't know about? He was getting around all right, but maybe he'd overexerted himself. Maybe he'd get sick now. Maybe—

"I wouldn't like that, either. If I think I'm going to die, I'll let you know."

"I'm not kidding."

He lifted his head, straightened slightly. "I know you're not kidding, Calla. I'm not going to die. Promise. I'm hurting a little bit right now, that's all. My ribs are bruised, I think."

She chewed her lip. Blood pumped warm inside her, the heat coming back to her fingers and toes. But he still looked pale and in pain.

But bruised ribs wouldn't kill him, and he'd warm up in time. He'd survived hypothermia the night before. He certainly wasn't hypothermic now, just very chilled. She had to deal with the situation a moment at a time, not borrow trouble. She could try insisting he go back to bed, get under the electric blanket again, not move the rest of the day. He might not cooperate. Fretting would do no good, and like most men, he didn't seem to want coddling or fussing. And she wasn't used to having anyone to coddle or fuss over.

The situation was one of a strange intimacy, and yet so very awkward at the same time.

"I'll go fix the chili," she said, standing. "And no arguing, all right? Let me do this. You've done enough."

"I wasn't going to argue," he answered.

She headed for the kitchen, stopped and looked back at him. He'd shut his eyes again. Chuck hadn't moved, as if he planned to stay there, watch the stranger—J.D.—for her. The parlor was a homey room, ordinary, stuffed with comfortably worn antiques. And one uncomfortably sexy stranger who was leaps and bounds beyond ordinary. She observed him for a moment without the pressure of him watching her back.

His dark hair was tousled from him dragging the wool cap off his head, making him look like he'd just woken up. Bed head. He even looked good with bed head, intensely masculine, sensually delicious. In repose, the hard planes of his face were softer, but the lines of fatigue and pain remained.

Working to dismiss the concern she could do nothing to allay, she forced her feet to take her to the kitchen where she set about preparing the chili. While the ground beef browned, she steadily chopped onions and peppers. She hadn't asked him if he liked it spicy.

She kept the hot peppers to a minimum just in case. She opened a couple cans of beans and popped the entire ingredient list into a big kettle on top of the stove. A few more minutes and she had corn bread made from stone-ground meal she bought from a local farmer in the oven. While the bread baked and the chili simmered, she methodically reviewed the goods in the pantry, what she had, what they could eat without cooking if they lost power and were snowbound indefinitely. She cleaned up the pan, bowl, and utensils she'd used to prepare the food.

Wiped the countertop.

Made more coffee.

Filled Chuck's doggy dish, which brought him running. Checked on the horses, and the kittens in the barn. She would have liked to bring the kittens inside, but she knew her fierce and protective mama cat wouldn't like that.

Busy, busy. She avoided checking on the stranger. Or thinking about J.D.

In case the generator went out and hot water didn't last all day, she decided a shower had better be next on her to-do list when she had the corn bread out, cooling on a wire rack. She gathered up a change of clothes, couldn't help taking a peek at him as she passed through the front room. The bathroom door clicked loud in the quiet farmhouse. She was on one side of a door, the sexy stranger on the other.

Calla leaned against the sink, took a deep breath, wondered if she needed a cold shower, not a hot one. What was wrong with her? She was hot.

Hot for a total stranger.

She felt achy, needy. Her body was crying out for sex. She hadn't had sex in a long, long time. An embarrassingly long time, if the truth were told. Brian had done a number on her but good. The marriage had been brief, but the echoes of its pain hadn't gone away. *You don't like sex*, he'd told her. *There's something wrong with you*, he'd told her.

Young and stupid, that's what she'd been. She'd fought within herself to feel desire for a man who'd turned into an emotional control freak after the wedding, who ordered sex like he was ordering from a menu even as he demeaned her by telling her she didn't like it. Everything she did, whether it was in bed or out, was wrong, wrong, wrong. She'd tried to make the marriage work.

Sometimes she still blamed herself that it hadn't. Divorce felt like a failure, even when her friends tried to tell her it was a triumph.

But she knew it had been more than Brian's fault. What if he was right? What if she didn't like sex?

She'd struggled periodically with that question, made some attempts to answer it in brief relationships right after the split. But work had always come first. Work had always been safer. And now,

since she'd left her life with Ledger Pharmaceuticals last year, she was even more isolated here on
the tree farm, more consumed by her new work
than she'd even been by the last. Determined not
to fail again, the way she'd failed at marriage, the
way she'd failed at Ledger. She ran her own ship
here. No one could tell her she was doing anything
wrong but her.

She would certainly never let a man in that
position again. Yet here she was feeling hot about
a total stranger. Even she, with her history of
mistakes, had enough sense to know that was a bad
idea.

She left the support of the sink, turned on the
water in the shower. She stripped her clothes
and stepped inside the curtained, tiled stall,
breathed in the hot, steaming air and started
shampooing her hair.

A few minutes later, her first clue was the
suddenly not-so-hot water.

Calla let loose a high-pitched scream as the
not-so-hot water pelting down on her turned a
shocking, freezing, almost painful ice-cold. She
grappled for the faucet handles even as the water
shut off on its own accord—whatever water had
been left in the system gone now, the well pump
dead. She pushed wildly at the shower curtain, just

wanting out, wanting a towel. Pounding. Someone was pounding on the bathroom door, calling her name. She gasped, swallowed hard, shivering, looking around blindly for a towel. The light was out, the windowless bathroom dark.

"I'm o—"

She didn't quite get the word *okay* out before the bathroom door burst open and she stood there, naked, in front of his shocked and worried and oh-so-noticing eyes.

Chapter 6

Calla was fine. She was quite obviously fine. She was way beyond fine, in fact. She was gorgeous and she was naked in the light that fell straight over into the dark bathroom. Dane would be lucky if he could ever wipe that image out of his head.

He jerked the door shut pronto, his heart pounding like a jackhammer gone berserk.

"I'm sorry," he said to the door. "I heard you scream—"

Yeah, and she'd screamed again when he'd barged into the bathroom.

"I called your name," he went on. "You didn't

answer." He'd freaked out. Completely. Totally. Freaked out.

He'd fallen into some wavery half sleep on the couch, woken to a really great smell coming from the kitchen and the sound of Calla screaming. Screaming. All that had popped into his head was that someone was trying to hurt her. Someone was trying to kill her.

And it was up to him to save her.

Now there were other things popping into his head. Calla's hair, dripping wildly around her, making her look like a water goddess. Calla's breasts, smooth and round with taut pink nipples. Calla's long legs, toned and perfect. The curve of her stomach, the dark curls at the V of her thighs.

He banged his forehead lightly into the door. Focus. Control. He needed both, badly.

"I was cold," he heard her say shakily through the door. "The water went freezing cold." There was a beat of silence, then she added, "The light's out. The generator must have gone dead."

Her voice was low, embarrassed. He didn't embarrass easily, but he was pretty sure he'd be embarrassed, too. Just as soon as other, more primal, reactions stopped throbbing through his body.

"I'm sorry," he said again.

She didn't answer then the door opened. He

stepped back, out of the way. She'd dressed quickly, in the dark, in jeans and a sweatshirt. Her hair lay wet, sticking to her cheeks, clinging to her shoulders. Her face was pink and she carefully avoided contact with his eyes. She stopped in the doorway as if she didn't know whether she wanted to come out or dart back inside.

"I shouldn't have screamed," she said. "I was cold, that's all. I didn't mean to scare you."

"I didn't mean to—" See her naked. Drive himself insane. Make the awkwardness of their situation even more awkward.

"Let's just forget it, okay?" She brushed past him, headed for the kitchen. He saw her flipping light switches up and down, as if hoping for a different reaction than the one she was getting if she just kept trying. Her shoulders sagged as he came up behind her. "The generator's dead," she said again. She turned, finally lifting her huge, wary eyes to his. "That's it." She shivered.

He had the intense urge to put his arms around her, remind her that they had prepared for this. But that wouldn't do his wayward body any good, and it might upset her. He couldn't move too fast in breaking down her barriers. And he definitely wasn't going to get intimate with her, not physically. The fact that he was even thinking about it wasn't good.

"We'll be all right," he said.

"Yeah. I know." But her voice sounded unsteady.

Her skin was still flushed from the shower and every breath he took filled his nostrils with the sweet misty heather scent of her body wash.

"Well, are you hungry now?" she asked, ducking around him to lift the lid off a large pot, stir it.

He nodded then remembered she couldn't see him. "Yes. Thank you." He wandered over, checking out the chili over her shoulder. "Smells great. I'll get a fire going." There was a fireplace in the kitchen, too, but he was thinking they should conserve fuel. "We should probably make camp in the front room," he suggested. "Focus on keeping us warm enough in there, not try to heat the whole house."

She turned, looked up at him with impossibly big eyes. "Good plan." She reached in a drawer, tossed a box of matches to him.

He got a fire going in short order and Calla joined him with bowls of hot chili, corn bread on the side, and a couple of glasses of water. He sat on the couch and she curled up on the rag rug on the floor. She was close to the fire and he realized she was still cold because of her damp hair that was starting to curl a little around her face.

"Sorry about feeding you chili for breakfast,"

she said. "I just wanted to fix something that would last us a while. I live by myself so I'm not used to thinking about anyone else when I'm cooking. I just fix whatever I feel like. Oh, and there's more coffee if you want some later."

She was single, or she seemed to be. He was curious. "No boyfriend?"

Lowering the spoon she'd brought up to her mouth, she said a flat, "No."

She took the bite and he watched her curiously, wondering just how much information he could get out of her. How much he should try to get out of her.

Two days. Forty-eight hours.

But how many of those hours would he be snowed in with her? They weren't just trapped in this house anymore. With the fireplace their only source of heat, they were trapped in this *room* now. He should take advantage of the opportunity.

They ate in silence for a few minutes.

"You mentioned your grandfather," he said, finishing up the chili and setting the bowl aside. Her family seemed like a safe way to circle around to more information about her current personal life. "You grew up here?"

"Not here as in on this farm." She set her bowl on the floor beside her, curled her knees up to her chest and held them with her arms. Her face was in profile, her fine features shadowed against the flames of the fire behind her. She turned her gaze back to him then. "I grew up in Haven, though. My father ran a family restaurant in town. My mom taught third grade."

"Your family's still around here?"

She shook her head. "My parents died in a car accident almost ten years ago."

He remembered that no immediate family had been at the trial other than some cousins. Now he knew why. A lot of friends had testified at the sentencing hearing. Calla Jones had a lot of friends.

"I'm sorry."

She looked down, picked at the cuff of her jeans. "It's okay. I still had my grandfather. We were close." She looked up again. "He died about a year and a half ago. About that time, I was ready to come back to Haven, so I took over the farm."

"Where were you before you came back to Haven?"

"I worked for Ledger Pharmaceuticals."

"Really?" He strove for a conversational tone. "What do they do? I mean, they sell drugs, I know that."

"They're a small company, but they do quite a

bit of pharmaceutical development. I was in basic research. I worked on cancer drugs."

"I'm impressed." The names of researchers had never been more than part of documentation to Dane before, part of his legal work in funneling paperwork to the FDA. He'd seen Calla's name before, as an associate on projects. She was the lead on one of the drugs working its way through the system now.

"Don't be."

"Why not?" She was beautiful, smart, educated. She had to be driven, too, or had been at some time.

"I got fired. I can't believe I told you that." She frowned.

"What happened?"

"I screwed up."

"You mean a drug didn't work out? Didn't do what it was supposed to do?"

"It was promising, but it had a major side effect." She shrugged as if it was no big deal, but it was obvious it was, to her, and that she blamed herself. "I was the project head. *First time* project head. It was for a drug we called setapraxin. Ledger had put a lot of money into the development, a lot of faith in me. I should have seen the possibility for trouble, but I missed it. I ran trials before I picked up on it, and it was a fundamental flaw. A fundamental flaw in my own research."

"Little hard on yourself?"

"You can't be easy on yourself when you're spending millions of dollars and people's lives are at stake. The drug would cure breast cancer, but it would also destroy heart function over time. I took full responsibility. Or, tried to. Unfortunately, my team got the ax, too. You don't spend that kind of money, blow it and not pay the price."

Setapraxin rang a bell. Maybe he'd picked up some company gossip without realizing it.

Carter Sloane was a hard taskmaster at Ledger, Dane knew that. He could also be kind and generous with employees, and he knew that, too. Carter had been the first and only person from Ledger who had come to his aid when he'd needed it, when he'd been arrested.

"I'm sorry," he said.

She shrugged. "It was meant to be. I was supposed to come back to Haven."

"And now you sell Christmas trees." It occurred to him that it was December 20 and there was no merrily decorated tree in the house. The cobbler with no shoes. "Where's *your* Christmas tree?"

"Well…" She sighed. "This is a secret, so don't tell anyone," she said conspiratorially, "but I don't like Christmas much. I mean, I like it—for other people. I love it for other people. I love to help make other people's Christmases better with a homegrown tree they can pick out, chop down. I make a whole event out of it here, just like Grandpa did. Serve cider and cookies and popcorn balls, give away packets of reindeer treats, and have sleigh rides out on the hill for everyone who buys a tree. It's fun. Especially the kids, seeing the kids' faces. But for me, no. I'm not that into it. I guess it's not the same without my family."

He wanted to tell her he didn't like Christmas, either, but suddenly the way she'd described the holiday activities that went on at Haven Christmas Tree Farm, he felt nostalgic for it, for the Norman Rockwell painting holiday she'd described.

Work, work, work. His job had meant everything to him. He'd called going to the gym a personal life. Relationships with women had always been brief and skin-deep. His life had seemed pretty barren, looking back on it from prison, though he'd rather have had his work-filled, barren life back than spend the rest of his life in jail.

Calla Jones's description made him want something a little bit more.

Focus, he reminded himself.

"I won't tell anyone," he said. "I wouldn't want you to end up with lumps of coal in your stocking."

She laughed then. "Oh, I'm pretty sure I'm already on Santa's bad list."

"And why would that be?" Now she had his curiosity piqued.

"I don't tell all my secrets." She pushed to her feet. "You want some coffee now?"

"I'll get it. You relax." He took her bowl from her before she could argue, and stacking it with his own, headed for the kitchen.

The farmhouse kitchen was already turning cool with the central heat gone. He set the bowls in the sink, poured out two cups of coffee and wondered what Calla's other secrets were.

She'd gotten off the floor and was curled up in the worn recliner when he went back to the front room. Outside, the wide front windows of the farmhouse revealed a gloomy white world through frost-laced panes. She lifted her head, slid her gaze up to his as he handed her a cup of coffee then sat down.

"Thanks," she said. "I'm glad you seem to be feeling better. I was pretty worried about you last night."

"I'm lucky you found me."

"Wasn't me. It was Chuck. I thought he was nuts. He raced off down the driveway to the road. I called him but he wouldn't come back. I would have just left his sorry butt and went on home but… I don't know. He seemed so insistent somehow. Like he knew you were there."

"I'm glad you didn't leave his sorry butt."

She gave a soft laugh. "I do love him. But he *is* a crazy dog sometimes. Usually he's after a cat. I guess I thought it might be one of the kittens down at the road, hurt or something. I've got a mama with kittens in the barn right now."

"You're not quite alone here at the farm then, are you?"

"Just the cats. Chuck. A couple horses. Luckily I was thinking ahead enough to put out plenty of feed in the barn, and they're tucked safe in their stalls. I'll have to check on them tomorrow, though." Her expression turned pensive.

Tomorrow was a mystery. Would the snow stop?

"You handle all this by yourself? The tree farm, all the holiday activities and events?" he asked. She was still wary, not revealing a lot, but he was getting there. Who else was in her life? It wasn't one of her animals who'd killed her, and the friends he'd seen at the sentencing hearing were unlikely suspects. Not that he was dismissing anyone.

"I've got a couple farmhands. Or, usually I do. They aren't real reliable."

This was interesting. He recalled the two farmhands at the trial. They'd had alibis, but Dane didn't put a lot of stock in that, not in a town as clannish as Haven. A guilty man could have a false alibi if an innocent man could have none at all.

"Anyway, except for the busy season right at the holidays, I do pretty good here by myself." She sounded proud of her independence, and maybe a little stubborn. "My grandfather ran the farm mostly on his own for sixty years. Right up till he died, and he was eighty-five. I can't complain." She furrowed her brow. "Really, I can't complain at all. Look at what's happened to you."

"I'm alive. Thanks to you."

"You don't know who you are. I can't even imagine that."

Guilt twisted in Dane's chest. He didn't want her feeling sorry for him. How would she react if he told her the truth? He was Dane McGuire from Ledger.

"Isn't it driving you crazy, the not knowing?"

Calla was saying. "What if there's someone out there, worried sick about you?"

He blinked, refocused on her face, tipped toward him curiously, concerned. He considered her question for a beat, considered how he could lie to her as little as possible. Lying to Calla Jones didn't feel good.

"I don't think so." Nope, there wouldn't be anyone worried sick about him.

"You don't know that."

"I'm not married. Apparently." He lifted his ringless finger.

"Not every man who's married wears a ring," she pointed out. "Especially if they don't want other people to know right offhand that they *are* married."

Was he imagining that bitter edge to her voice?

"I'd like to think I'm not a complete ass," he answered.

She made a sound that was almost a laugh, but not quite.

"Sorry. I didn't mean to suggest you were."

"Have you ever been married?" he asked, suspicious that he already knew the answer based on her comments that she wasn't interested in men.

"Once. Years ago. He *was* a complete ass. So that job's taken anyway."

"I'm glad you're not bitter," he cracked gently. There was pain flaring in her eyes. He didn't like that. He felt protective of Calla Jones suddenly, and not in the physical sense.

"Me, too." Now she did laugh.

"So is that what you're doing buried up here on a mountain making other people's Christmases merry instead of your own?"

She sobered. "I don't think of it that way."

"Maybe you should. You're a very pretty woman, Calla. What are you doing hiding up here alone?" He'd gone too far. He'd stepped over a line, he saw it immediately. He didn't know her well enough to make judgments about her personal life or offer unsolicited advice. And considering his own personal life, his comment certainly fell into the "pot calling the kettle black" category.

Or was it calling her pretty that bothered her? He wasn't sure. Most women liked compliments....

"I like my life just fine." Her words were stiff. "I'm not hiding. I enjoy helping families celebrate the holidays, make them more special. Doesn't mean there's anything wrong with my own life just because I don't have a Christmas tree up for myself."

"I know. I'm sorry. I didn't mean to offend. I don't ever put up a tree, either."

Exactly what he'd said didn't register till he saw the shock on her face.

Chapter 7

"You remember that?" Calla's pulse kicked as she watched J.D. He looked as shocked as she felt.

He didn't say anything for a long beat. "That just popped out. I wasn't thinking."

Suddenly she remembered that she didn't trust him. Not one bit. What if he was lying to her?

He could be a criminal for all she knew. What kind of naive fool was she to be sitting here chatting with him like he was a neighbor she'd invited in for supper? Telling him her secrets? He was sitting here telling her she was pretty. Just what did he have in mind?

She was letting her guard down, big-time.

She'd never put much stock in the "positive ions triggering otherworldly events" nonsense that had overtaken the town recently, but her behavior with J.D.—John Doe the Stranger—was certainly out of this world for her. And if she could put it down to the ability of the earthquake-induced positive ions to supposedly induce the incredible, that would be nice, but she knew it was something a lot more visceral.

Like that whole putting him on a cracker and eating him fantasy.

She swallowed hard. "Well, good. Maybe you'll remember more. I hope so."

Did she? Part of her certainly did, but part of her had really started getting into the sexy, mysterious stranger aspect of this snowbound *fantasy*. She could indulge in a little harmless lust, couldn't she? Everyone deserved a fantasy life. Only it wasn't really a fantasy, this being trapped with him. It was real.

She needed to snap out of it. Pronto. Before he got the wrong impression and things stopped being harmless.

"Maybe it would help if you rest. Or, do whatever you want to do. Make yourself at home, okay? I've got work."

"In a blizzard?"

"I don't mean outside." She pushed up from the recliner. "If I have any luck at all, the roads will clear by the weekend and I can still do some business. This is the last big choose-and-cut weekend before Christmas. Pray for plows." She managed to sound optimistic and casual.

I like my life just fine. Maybe that was true and maybe it wasn't.

"Maybe I can help. I don't need to rest." He stood.

"I told you, I manage around here fine on my own. I don't need help. I don't need a Christmas tree, and I don't need you."

He froze in his tracks. The look on his lean, fire-shadowed face told her he was confused. Well, good. So was she. Casual hadn't lasted long, had it? He sparked baffling longings she'd thought had died inside her, longings for something more than fantasy, mixed with a whole lot of trepidation and distrust.

"I'll stay out of your way," was all he said.

Great. Now she felt like a jerk. Maybe that was better than feeling like a fool, though.

She'd take it.

The rest of the house was chilling down fast, but she didn't let that bother her. He'd been right about focusing their limited fuel on one room.

She just didn't want to share that room with him every second of the day.

She went to the spare bedroom and opened up a box of clear bags and several more boxes filled with the various goods she used to make up the reindeer food packets she gave out at the choose-and-cuts. Corn, oats, raisins, nuts, sort of a granola-for-reindeer mix for kids to put on their doorsteps or driveways when Santa stopped by to deliver presents. She imagined it made the birds and squirrels happy on Christmas morning. Each bag would be tied up tightly with a piece of twine.

The house was achingly quiet. She rummaged for a Christmas CD and jabbed it into a battery-powered player. "Frosty the Snowman" music covered up the silence that was uncomfortable even when she was alone. Maybe especially when she was alone. She didn't want to think and J.D. was making her think. And feel. And a few other things she hadn't done lately.

Sitting cross-legged in the cold room, she filled and tied bags, hoping she'd actually get to give them out this weekend. Her fingers got numb from the cold. Childish and stupid, that's what she was. Working back here in a cold room, making way more reindeer bags than she could possibly use this weekend.

Childish and stupid and… Paranoid. She *was* hiding. She didn't have any solid reason not to trust J.D. other than that he was a man.

She got off the bed, fisting her cold hands under her arms as she crossed them over her chest. She was really making this way more complicated than it had to be.

Heading for the front room from the tiny side hall, she found it empty.

She checked the kitchen, and the bathroom. Music from the CD player filtered across the house. Snow swirled thickly outside. Blood pumped in her veins.

Where'd he go?

She padded quickly in her sock feet back through the house, realized the door to her own bedroom was shut. Maybe the stranger had decided to rest, after all, though if he was resting in the cold bedroom rather than the warm parlor, he really was nuts. He had seemed out of his head earlier even though he'd seemed to stabilize.

Pushing the door inward, she froze, the blood pumping loud in her ears now.

"What do you think you're doing?" she demanded.

* * *

Dane jerked, his knuckles hitting the top of the drawer he'd opened in Calla's sidetable. Snooping wasn't an answer she'd like.

Though it would be the truth.

"I was looking for something to read," he said, thinking quickly. "I didn't want to bother you."

"So you just thought you'd go through my personal things, looking for a book?"

"I figured the nightstand was a good place to look. I'm sorry. It was out of line. I just thought you'd rather I didn't bother you."

She stood there, poised for battle, her cheeks flushed—this time with anger. After a few seconds' pause, she visibly relaxed.

"I'm sorry. I was…a little curt with you earlier. I'm not having a very good day, I guess."

"You're having a blizzard and you're worried about your business. You're allowed to be upset about it. I'm rummaging around on my own and you're allowed to be upset about that, too. I'm not being a very good guest, especially since I'm an uninvited one. I should have been patient and waited for you to finish working."

"No. It's okay. I told you to make yourself at home, didn't I?"

Yes, she had, but not in her nightstand, where

he hadn't found any books but had found an envelope of pictures. The envelope was addressed to Calla, postal-stamped a few weeks earlier, no return address, and nothing inside but another envelope filled with pictures and a sticky note attached to the front. The note had read: *Just ran across these pictures and thought you'd want to have them.* The pictures were a little faded, a mix of scenery that looked as if they'd been taken on a road trip. Some of them included Calla and a man, both of them young, smiling, clearly in love.

The ex? Or a man from some other relationship? Hard to guess if she was saving them sentimentally or had just shoved them in a drawer to get them out of the way. Either way, she hadn't thrown them out, so they meant something to her in some way.

Otherwise, he hadn't come across much of interest. Her kitchen drawers had revealed nothing but ordinary utensils and bills and the usual odd, useless items pushed to the back. The bedroom hadn't revealed much more—mainly the expected personal items that had made him feel like a heel to be touching.

There was little evidence of her business life in the house, though apparently she utilized the second bedroom for work space. He didn't have much excuse to get into that room.

"I'd rather help you than read," he said. "I'd be happy to make myself useful, to pay you back."

"That's not necessary." Or wanted, apparently. She still looked and sounded stiff, as if he made her uncomfortable. So much for making any headway at getting closer to her. "I'm finished. There really isn't a lot I can do today. I'd do some paperwork, but my office is in the barn and I'm not going to try to get out there in this."

The snow was really coming down now, and while it wasn't quite noon, the day was darker than it had been first thing in the morning. The light coming through the window was dull and gray. Wind howled around the house, and he heard a tree limb crash outside, not far. Calla jumped.

He didn't think. He just reached out for her then and dropped his hands back when he saw the flash of new panic in her eyes.

Damn if he hadn't felt some of that panic himself, and it shouldn't bother him that she felt it, too. It would be wiser for both of them to keep their distance in spite of the powerful surge of attraction that hit him whenever he looked at her.

"All we need is for a tree to crash through the roof," she said, focusing on the external event rather than the unspoken internal thing that had happened next. She shuddered.

"Think positive. It hasn't happened so far."

"So far would be the key words."

"No sense borrowing trouble," he said.

"No, I guess not. We have enough already."

Her list of trouble included him, he was certain. His list of trouble included murder... And her. Definitely her, too. She wasn't like any of the women he'd been attracted to in the past.

She was different. More real, even in this strangely surreal day.

And she scared the crap out of him. He could get in deep with her if circumstances were different, and he'd never done that before or even thought about it. He didn't do attachments, not even with family.

His parents were currently away on an expedition to a remote Pacific island to study one of the world's last untouched societies. Primitive sociology had always been their consuming interest, not their son.

He followed her out to the front room. A log fell in the fire, sending up a spray of sparks. She knelt in front of the hearth, added another log, used the tongs to rearrange the wood then moved a couple of knickknacks off an old chest at the end of the couch. She pulled out a stack of dog-eared westerns.

"What do you like to read?" she asked when

she turned, straightened, faced him where he stood in the middle of the room. "Westerns okay?"

Was this a trick question? "I don't know. I was just bored," he said. "Anything is fine."

"My grandfather was a big western fan. There's boxes of them in the attic, too." She pushed a handful of them at him.

Their fingers met, then their eyes, in one of those paralyzing moments that seemed to charge the air with electricity. A drift of fear swept across her gaze, too. She put her hands back to her sides.

Even accidentally invading her personal space seemed to be a problem for her. Why?

"Look, I'm no good at this." Her arms crossed over her waist, defensive. She stood in front of the fireplace as if undecided whether she was going to go or stay.

"No good at what?"

"Social niceties. I'm a loner, I guess. I'm not hiding up here," she repeated her earlier denial. "I'm just more comfortable living alone. I've always worked alone, or as alone as possible when working on a lab team. I was an only child. I was a failure at marriage. I don't host parties, other than what I do for my business. I hardly ever even invite anyone over."

"You have friends."

Her gaze tightened. "How would you know?"

"Just guessing. You're a kind, generous, beautiful woman. Why wouldn't you have friends?"

She looked embarrassed. "Okay, yes, I have friends. Old friends. From kindergarten."

Was that how long it took her to trust someone? Twenty-five years?

"I'm just saying that this is very awkward for me," she said. "I'm not comfortable. In fact, I'm really *uncomfortable*. I don't know you, and here we are, stuck in this house until the plows get here." She blew out a long breath, tense. "I guess I'm just trying to be honest. I don't want you to think I'm some kind of freak or something, but I don't know what to do with you."

His lips curved of their own volition. "I don't think you're a freak, social or otherwise. And you don't have to do anything with me. You don't have to do anything other than what you want to do. I certainly don't expect anything from you."

She studied him. "Those are nice words."

"I mean them."

"Maybe. You *are* a man."

He frowned. "I don't understand."

"I just want to be clear about something," she said.

"And what is that, exactly?"

Her expression revealed an endearing mix of awkwardness and persistence. She was trying to tell him something and having a hard time getting it out. He wanted to blame the craziness of his situation for how bad he wanted to know what she was going to say next. Or maybe the fact that his entire future hinged on finding out everything he could about her.

But he knew it was far more than that. He just didn't know what it was.

She took a deep breath as if fortifying herself. "Well, and I'm a woman."

"I'm a man. You're a woman. I think we're both clear on that." He saw her lips tighten and he said, "I'm not making fun of you, I promise."

"When men and women are alone together, it's not exactly unusual for them to start thinking about certain things," she went on in a rush, determined. "Stupid things."

"Like what?" Now he was being difficult, but he couldn't resist her.

She blew out a noisy breath. "Like sex."

"Are you afraid you're going to sleep with me just because we're snowed in together?" he asked.

Calla forced herself to meet the stranger's gaze even while it made her stomach stumble all over again. The whole line of conversation was achingly embarrassing. She was an idiot, a complete dolt. She didn't know why she'd thought airing this issue would make it easier to be in the house with him. She liked him even though she had no reason to trust him, and she was definitely lusting after him and his wide shoulders and hard chest and lean good looks and bafflingly nice eyes.

And then he'd had to go and say she was beautiful.

It had been a while since she'd done something stupid and rash with a man, but she knew her own history. And there was something frighteningly magnetizing about the way he looked at her.

The heat burning her face could have peeled off skin. "I just wanted to get it out in the open," she said. "We're two adults, both apparently single. This is like a soap opera scenario, you know."

"No, I don't know. I don't watch soaps."

"Well, I used to. You tell me I'm beautiful and then what happens next is we haul a mattress out here. We get naked to share body heat and snuggle under the covers together in front of the fire. Then we have sex."

Amnesia was just a bonus plot point.

"Are we going to do that?" He was laughing. He was actually laughing. "I didn't know it was that easy."

"I didn't say we were going to do that!"

"You're stamping your foot again."

Really? She was, she realized. She controlled her feet with an effort and worked on steadying her racing pulse. "No, I'm not."

J.D. ignored the obvious lie. "So what are our other options?"

"Well, you could turn out to be a horror movie killer. You could get an ax and chop me up, or slice me to shreds with some of the knives in the kitchen."

Maybe she was just getting out all her deepest fears here. Air them aloud. They seemed, and sounded, silly, out loud and oddly that did make her feel better in spite of the embarrassment.

"I promise I'm not going to do that," he said. "Though I don't blame you for worrying about it. You're a woman alone, and that makes you vulnerable. You should be very careful. More careful than you probably are."

He was serious, she realized. The concern that darkened his eyes actually sent a prickle along the back of her neck.

"Well, I'm safe for now," she said, shrugging off the eerie feeling. "In horror movies, the girl always has sex first then she dies."

"I could just turn out to be a decent guy who

happened to be rescued from a snowstorm by a nice woman," he suggested.

"Isn't that an oxymoron?"

Quizzical, and yes, dammit, sexy brow raised. Could he be any more gorgeous?

"What?"

"Decent and guy in the same sentence."

"Man-hater, are you?"

Was she? Maybe. She didn't want to be. Maybe blaming an entire gender for her problems wasn't the tippy top of taking personal responsibility, and she was big on taking responsibility. Sometimes, maybe, she took too much responsibility, and the way she'd handled things at Ledger had left her feeling pretty raw and low the past year. She was human. She made mistakes. Being fired had been an extreme repercussion, but she had accepted it.

If Ledger just left her alone now, she'd be happy, but her name was still on drugs in the FDA process, so she knew that was a pipe dream, at least for a while.

Some lawyer from Ledger had called just the other day. Some form missing from her file they wanted her to sign. She just wished they'd go away so she could get on with her new life and forget about the old one.

"I'm just nervous. I do stupid things when I'm

nervous. I say stupid things, too." She felt desperate for a change of subject.

"I don't want to make you nervous, Calla." He glanced at the stack of books in his hands, picked one out and set the rest on the couch. "I think you're pretty. That doesn't mean I have no self-control. Do I look at you and think, wow? Yes, I do. But I'm not going to do anything about it, not unless you want me to. I don't know what kind of men you're used to, but you're safe with me, I promise. I'm going to read. You don't have to entertain me, you know."

He stretched out on the couch and cracked open the book. She sank into the recliner and stared at the fire, trying to forget he was there. Fat chance, but she could pretend. *Do I look at you and think, wow? Yes, I do.*

The compliment still had her pulse leaping. A decent guy? Maybe he was. He'd been nothing but kind and polite, and just because he was truly drool-worthy didn't eliminate the possibility that he was a decent human being.

She was the one who'd brought up the totally inappropriate topic of sex just so she could tell him he wasn't getting any. It wasn't anything he'd said or done that was unnerving her. It was her reaction to him.

Maybe it was a little of the old Christmas lonelies that tended to hit her this time of year. She'd used the business last year to cover it up. Restless energy was now burning her from the inside out.

Her stranger didn't seem plagued by the same. As wind swept around the house again and the fire crackled and spit, he calmly turned a page in the book, seemingly absorbed.

Calla felt like she was going to go stark-raving mad. She was tired and far too keyed-up to nap.

She made a concerted effort to relax, from the toes up. Sinking further into the recliner, she put her head back, closed her eyes, willed her pulse to slow down.

That she slept was the first miracle.

That the tree that crashed down on top of the house didn't kill her was the second one.

Chapter 8

Dane was totally unprepared for the disaster, despite the earlier warning of the possibility when a huge limb had fallen near the farmhouse. Calla's farmhouse hadn't been destroyed on December 22 when he'd arrived to conduct Ledger business with her. The house had been in normal condition.

It certainly hadn't had a massive hole in the roof.

He'd come back in time to change the past.

Had his mere presence changed the past already? Obviously it had. He hadn't even been in Haven this time last year.

Here he'd been calmly expecting everything to

go as it had before. Afraid everything *would* go as it had before, but thinking at least that he had certain guarantees. Maybe what he really had to fear was that things were not going to go as they had before—and he was going to be completely unprepared to save Calla from murder, not to mention Mother Nature.

All of that raced through his shocked mind as he lunged across the room, grabbing Calla into his arms, pulling her back as a huge chunk of tree followed the even huger chunk of roof colliding with the inside of her house. He rolled, cradling her close. Her entire body was trembling. She was terrified.

There was another crashing sound as part of the roof broke off, settled inside, and she tangled herself so tightly around him, he didn't know where he stopped and she began other than his bruised ribs that were screaming in discomfort.

His heart pounded, hard, and he could feel her heart pounding, too. He could hear her short, gaspy breaths.

There was a hole in the roof.

Cold crept across his consciousness as silence settled, lengthened. Wind picked up, and through the hole in the roof, thick gray light illuminated a steady fall of snow. Snow that was falling straight into the house now.

Accumulation from the roof was in the parlor already. The fire was out, the fireplace blocked by debris.

"Calla?"

She didn't answer. In the interest of breathing, he worked to pry her off him. He'd rolled them to the edge of the room, hoping the supports would hold there, that the roof would only cave in the weaker center portion where the tree had struck. That had worked. For now.

"Are you okay?" he asked. He'd managed to loosen her grip on him just enough for him to see her face. Pale, shocked, terror-filled.

"I'm okay." She didn't sound okay, but she was trying. "Where's Chuck?"

"I don't know."

The shine in her eyes told him she was holding back tears, big-time, then there was a scratching sound on the wood floor of the hall and the dog, thank God, bounded at her, wriggling between them. Calla did cry then, sitting up, arms grabbing the dog tightly to her chest.

"Can you stand?"

She nodded, blinking back the tears still falling. He took her hand, pushing up from the floor, pulling her with him. He could feel the shaking of her hand, knew her knees had to be shaking, too. Hell, his were. The roof had collapsed, nearly on top of them. They could have died.

They weren't in real good shape as it was.

"Kitchen," he said. "There's a hearth in there. We need to keep warm." Food, water, fire. Everything they needed. They were still all right.

Except, he realized as they got to the kitchen, there was no door to shut between the kitchen and the now open-to-the-elements front room. The dog padded after them.

"We're going to need a hammer and nails," he said. "We've got to hang something up over the door frame to keep out the cold."

"Okay." She looked and sounded like she was operating on automatic, and maybe it was a good thing to keep her busy. She'd slept for a couple hours, and woken to a new nightmare. She was in shock. He headed to the bedroom and grabbed the linens and blankets off the bed, stepped over debris, dumped them on the kitchen floor and then went back.

She stood there, staring at him when he came back.

Dane shoved the top mattress off the bed the last few feet into the room, shoving it in front of the kitchen hearth.

*What happens next is we haul a mattress out
here. We get naked to share body heat and snuggle
under the covers together in front of the fire. Then
we have sex.*

He had to work to push away that very visual
and sensual impression from her earlier comments.

"I don't know about you, but those chairs don't
look real comfortable if we're talking about
spending the night here." He nodded toward the
wooden cane-back chairs at the kitchen table.
"I'm not playing soap opera games with you,
Calla. We've got to make it through the night and
I don't see us getting much rest on the hard floor."

"I know." She swallowed visibly. "I found the
hammer and nails."

"All right." He took the flat white sheet from the
bed and together he and Calla worked to hold and
nail it to the top of the door frame that led to the
front room, blocking the icy air. She got some
wide packing tape next and after going out again
for pillows and the radio from the bedroom, he
taped down the sides. "We might need to get out
there to get something else later," he pointed out.
For now, he'd secured the kitchen as best as could
be done under the circumstances. "Let's get the
fire going."

Calla dug up a new box of matches from a kitchen drawer while he carried an extra pile of wood in from the utility room. There were newspapers in a stack near the hearth and she crumpled several sheets, laying them in the wood. The fire finally lit, he sat back, looked at her again. And God, she was something to look at, her eyes humongous, lips parted, pulse beating wildly at her throat....

Yeah, he definitely looked at her and thought, wow. Every time.

"We're going to be okay," she said, as if convincing herself.

"I'm sorry about your roof."

She didn't speak right away. He had a feeling she couldn't, that the emotional reaction was too close to the surface. She was perched on the edge of the mattress, leaning over her knees toward the warmth of the fire.

"It's just a house, and not even the whole house, right?" she said softly, her profile showing the tremble in her mouth that was echoed in her voice. "But hey, I was so lucky earlier this year when we had an earthquake. I had some damage to the barn, but not too bad. There was a lot of damage in town, and there was one house out in the community that completely collapsed.

I've just got part of the roof down. I can get it fixed. It's my fault. I should have had that tree taken down last summer. I didn't want to spend the money then and now it'll cost a lot more."

The exposure to the blizzard wasn't going to do her house any good in the meantime, but he didn't need to remind her of that. She was doing her best to be brave in the face of disaster.

Dane didn't pay a lot of attention to the news, but her mention of the earthquake niggled at his consciousness, then leaped full-blown into his brain. There'd been some kind of nonsense about the quake triggering paranormal activity. Nearly a hundred miles away in Parkersburg, and sparing little time to follow current events, he hadn't missed that ruckus in the press on the heels of what certainly had been a news event of enough proportion that even he had noted coverage of it and had felt the distant rocking of the earth. *Anything could happen in Haven.* He remembered dismissing it at the time.

He was in Haven now, wasn't he? *Anything could happen…*

The prickly feeling he'd experienced before traced up his spine again. If what had happened to him wasn't paranormal activity, he didn't know what was.

He looked at Calla, her arms wrapped tightly around her bent knees. She lifted her gaze, stared back at him. This whole episode equaled an unbelievable nightmare. One sleepy little mountain town, a blinding blizzard, a creeping sense of the supernatural, and a murderer lurking somewhere.

Who could, quite frankly, strike anytime.

All it took to put all the pieces in place was for him to be on Calla's farm. The date wasn't written in stone. No guarantees. No one had handed him a playbook.

"I'm scared," she said suddenly, her voice very small.

Join the party, he thought grimly. "I'm here," he said. "I'm not going anywhere."

She almost laughed, but the sound came out choked.

He felt his heart catch. He hadn't felt so much for another person in he couldn't remember how long. Maybe never. He didn't spend enough time with other people outside work, personal time, to feel much at all.

"I'm glad you're here," she said quietly.

"Me, too. It's cold out there."

She smiled, and it took his breath.

"I'm sorry I treated you like you were some

kind of jerk here to attack me one way or another," she said. "That wasn't very nice of me."

"I don't want to hurt you, Calla. And you have every right to be careful about letting anyone, especially a strange man, into your house. You don't need to apologize for it."

His entire life had been about *not* making ties, but he was so very glad that he was here for her now, and not just because saving her life could mean saving his. If they got through this, if both of them got through this, was there a chance he could get to know her better, maybe?

That notion stole his breath away again and he pulled back, hard, with the entire train of thought. He'd lied to her from the moment he'd woken up. He'd been wrong. He knew now he could trust her, just felt it, visceral, deep down. But he had a story to tell that was impossible to believe, and add to that the fact that he'd already lied to her.

Just when she might be starting to trust him, a little bit, was not the time to throw her a curveball. Not if he wanted to save her life.

"Are you hungry?" he said, changing the subject abruptly.

She nodded. "Yeah. I guess so. You?"

He shook his head. "You go ahead." The adrenaline that had driven him through the crisis had passed and the throbbing pain in his ribs was taking precedence. A wave of exhaustion hit him at the same time. "I need to lie down, okay?"

Her brow knit. "Of course it's okay." She chewed her lip, watching him as he gingerly stretched out on the mattress. She leaned toward him, inadvertently jiggling what he imagined to be the most perfect breasts on the planet through the sweatshirt she wore. "Does it hurt?"

Maybe he *was* a jerk. He was feeling some discomfort in a totally separate area from his ribs. She had a body that wouldn't quit and an artlessly sexy way of carrying it. And he was male enough to notice.

"Yeah, it hurts," he said.

"You're not running a fever, are you?" She placed her cool, soft fingers on his forehead. Her gaze met his, her eyes dark with a flare of awareness he couldn't miss. Then she took a deep breath and backed off. "You feel okay."

"I'll be fine. I think I just need to get a little sleep."

"Do you want something, some more pain reliever?"

She'd given him some over-the-counter stuff earlier. "Maybe in a little while," he said.

"Okay. I'll be here."

"Where would you go?" he teased her, tired but still, dammit, so attracted to her no matter how wrong it might be.

Her head cocked and she studied him, her eyes clouded now with some emotion…nerves, maybe? The moment was gone, the awareness, replaced by that distant, careful woman who preferred to be alone against the world. He was starting to see beneath that shell of hers, to the hurting person inside, to a woman who was very, very vulnerable. Who had been so hard on her that she was so hard on herself?

"Go to sleep, J.D.," she said quietly.

Back to the business of survival.

She wouldn't let him in easily.

Chapter 9

Calla woke shivering. It took her a moment to realize where she was. On a mattress, on the floor, in her kitchen.

With a stranger.

Dull gray light filtered into the room. The hearth was cold, nothing but embers smoldering. They'd taken turns during the night, and it was on her second watch that she'd fallen asleep and let the fire die.

She turned her head abruptly, searching for him, a choked sob of relief filling her throat when she saw him. How dependent she had become on him, this stranger. He kept her from being alone. He exuded a confidence that made her think they could get through anything.

He was fast asleep, still. His lashes were long and dark, his nose straight. His hair fell over his forehead, making him look younger than she would guess him to be.

Without a doubt, he was one of the sexiest men she'd ever met. And nice. She kept thinking he would stop being nice, but he just kept proving her wrong.

She couldn't resist. She looked her fill, didn't want to take her eyes off him. She'd thought of nothing but him all night, even dreamed about him.

In his sleep, he must have kicked the blanket away. It tangled at his feet. She reached down, pulled it up, indulged in one more minute of looking at him, only that wasn't enough. She wanted to touch him.

Under her hand, the hard lines and unforgiving muscles of his chest were irresistible. She let her fingertips wander, lightly, as she pretended to do nothing but tuck the blanket more securely about him.

She wanted to touch him more, and she let her hand linger, reluctant to withdraw it. She thought of how it might feel if he touched her back, what it might be like to snuggle up with him on this cold, cold morning. What it would be like to trust a man, him, that much. How lovely that would be.

Her gaze lifted to his face and her pulse fluttered wildly as his eyes—open—stared straight back at her.

"Hi," she said stupidly.

"Hi." His voice came out rough from sleep. Sexy-rough.

She jerked her hand back, tucked it safely in her lap, but she couldn't pull her gaze away from his. It was like he held her in some kind of force field, though she was starkly aware that it was a voluntary surrender on her part. *Do I look at you and think, wow? Yes, I do.* His earlier comment bounced around her mind.

He found her attractive, he'd told her that much. But he hadn't made a single move. That could, she realized, drive her insane. Wanting him. Knowing he wanted her. Realizing he was so freaking nice that he would do nothing about it.

Really, she was starting to wonder if she might have made him up. Maybe she was dreaming.

"It's morning," she said. "I let the fire go out," she added guiltily. "It's cold. I'm sorry."

"You don't have to apologize," he said.

"It was just dumb," she said.

He studied her, seeming baffled by her self-blame. "It's no big deal. We were both sleeping. We can get the fire going again."

He wasn't going to yell at her. He wasn't going to tell her she was stupid and wrong and bad in so many ways. He just wasn't going to do a damn thing she expected a man to do. In every aspect of how he treated her, he was different.

Well, she knew men could be nice. Her grandfather had been wonderful. But she was pretty sure the universe had broken that mold after him.

Yet here was this kind, patient, calm, respectful man who'd landed, nearly literally, on her doorstep. Like a gift. It couldn't have been better unless he'd been naked and wrapped with a bow. *Santa's being good to you this year, Calla.*

That thought was so preposterous, she tried to choke back a laugh she would be way too embarrassed to explain, and failed. She slammed her hand to mouth then, tried to turn the laugh into a cough.

"What's so funny?" he asked.

Bummer. He hadn't missed that.

"Um, I can't explain. Forget it."

"I'm curious."

"Forget it!" She pushed up on her palms, leaned forward to grab a log, then another, and turned her attention fully on the fire.

He got up, too, and helped.

"You're feeling better?" she asked.

"Lots," he said.

She sat back on her heels. "Good. I'm glad." She smiled, and he smiled, too. A wide, sexy, heart-stopping smile that nearly gave her a heart attack.

"So what are we going to do today?" he asked.

Her stomach fluttered strangely. "Um… I need to check on the horses and the cats in the barn. Make sure everyone's got plenty of feed. If it stops snowing, and it looks like it's going to, I'll start shoveling out the driveway. When the plows come, I'll want to be ready to get the truck out. And later, if the roads are cleared, people might even come out for trees. I have to be ready, just in case."

"I can help you do that."

"You're—"

"Better," he reminded her. "Lots." He gave her a hard look from under those lashes that would make any woman jealous. He looked disgustingly delicious. "I plan on helping."

The snow cover on the hills glistened like a fairyland, drifts piled high against the fences. The field of pines was decorated by Mother Nature.

After a quick breakfast of coffee heated in an iron kettle over the kitchen fire and some fruit, they put their jackets on and Dane followed Calla outside. The snowfall was down to a light flurry, getting lighter all the time.

"Plows'll get out today," she said hopefully, turning back to look at him as she reached the bottom of the back steps they'd shoveled out as they'd left the house. Her breath came out visible in the cold air, her cheeks and nose prettily pink. She held a box of packaged reindeer treats in her arms and he carried another. Chuck bounced in circles around her.

Dane stood at the bottom of the steps in her grandfather's jacket and wondered what he was doing here. Everything that had happened this go-round in the past was giving him greater opportunity to spend time with Calla, to get to know Calla.

Which would only make it worse if she then died.

Could there be more to his purpose here in the past?

Under normal conditions, he might have noticed Calla. What man wouldn't? But he wouldn't have tried to get close to her. He'd been too busy with work, and too accustomed to what he'd only recently acknowledged had been a barren emotional life. No one to even care if he went to prison for the rest of his days other than his employer. It hadn't said much about him that was good.

And now… How could he even consider letting himself get attached to a woman who didn't know the truth about who he was, how he'd come to be here and he might well end up dead and soon if he couldn't stop it.

Calla didn't even seem to *want* the attraction that was all too obviously burning between them. But she felt it, he knew she did. And so did he. Was it just physical desire? He didn't think so, but he didn't want to risk using her that way, even if she would allow it. And she was vulnerable, despite her careful guard.

She was looking at him now, eyes wide, as if she could almost read his mind, then she turned, headed for the barn, her boots stamping with effort through the thick snow.

"Well?" She turned back to him. "Are you coming or not?"

He couldn't help smiling. He liked how direct she could be at times. He liked *her*. "I'm coming," he said.

The barn was big and red and antiquey enough to have a weather-worn Mail Pouch Tobacco emblem painted on the side. The way the land lay, the barn perched on a rise over the road where it curled this direction across her property. The two-lane highway coming across the mountain out of Haven was nothing but a ribbon of white. Bare-branched tree limbs swayed with icicles in the woods across the road.

Pine wreaths and swags decorated the doors and windows of the barn to welcome Christmas tree farm customers, and inside he found part of the barn had been set aside for business purposes. There was a table set up with foam cups and a hot water dispenser. Packets of hot chocolate, tea, cider and flavored coffees filled a basket. Bags of peppermints sat to one side. There were a few folding chairs leaned up against a wall, and a counter with an antique cash register. There was a door behind the counter marked Office.

She dumped the reindeer treat bags into a big, old-fashioned metal washtub on the floor. Iron shelving sported wrapped scented soaps, and canning jars held what appeared to be homemade candles. The soaps and candles were marked for sale.

"Do you make these?" he asked, curious.

She nodded. "Just a hobby, mostly. But people buy them, mostly when they're here getting trees. They make great last-minute Christmas gifts. I'm always ready for someone who might be desperate." She laughed. "But sometimes people come by during the year to buy, and I keep some in a consignment shop on the square in Haven, too."

Inside the barn, it was dark but for the light coming in some side windows and from the door they'd left open. She pulled the flashlight out of her pocket.

"Very industrious," he commented.

She shrugged. "I need an income year-round. I do a lot of other stuff, too."

"Like?"

"Festivals and fairs. I set up booths, sell my soaps and candles. All over the state. And I do a big pumpkin patch here in the fall—and pass out flyers then to remind people about the trees. Grandpa always did that, too, and it's something of a tradition around here to get pumpkins on the farm. I don't make a lot, but it all adds up and it's enough. The farm was paid for a long time ago. I just have to earn enough to keep it going. Luckily I have insurance to pay for the damage to the roof, and I'm sure there's going to be a lot of water damage in the house." She sighed. "But the house will be okay. It's been here a hundred years. It's not going anywhere on my watch." He could see her commitment in the set of her jaw.

"It's been in your family that long?" He

couldn't imagine. His own family tree included moves all over the place, even for his grandparents, and the longest he'd ever stayed in one place as a kid was at boarding school. His parents had been busy globe-trotting then, too.

She nodded. "Longer than that," she said. "My family goes back here about two hundred years. I've got cousins all over the place. I'm probably related to half the people in this county."

He didn't even know his cousins.

"Come on." She reached out, tugged his arm. "I can't wait to see my babies. I'm worried about them."

Dane grabbed a peppermint as she led him back into the barn. There were several stalls and the scent of dirt and tack and horse carried on the air, mixed with the sweet scent of Calla and the strangely erotic pleasure of her hand gripping his arm in a burst of excitement that seemed to keep her from realizing she was touching him. Her eyes shone in the shadows.

"That's Flash. And that's Lily. Grandpa named Lily for me."

It took him a second to work that out. "Calla lily."

"Right."

She moved her hand, dug into her pocket again

for the peppermints she'd stuck there while the horses leaned their heads over the stall door. They were gorgeous animals, dark coats with white spots.

"What kind of horses are they?"

"Appaloosas," she explained. "Aren't they beautiful?" She'd opened the stall door now, stepped inside. He watched her stroke each one then give them a peppermint treat from her hand before she went about the business of filling the grain bins. "Their water's frozen," she said. "We're going to have to go back, get some of the water from the house. Let's go check on the cats first." She shut the stall and peeked into the next one. Then the next one. "Here they are. She moves them all the time."

A mama calico cat, her eyes bright yellow in the brief dash of the flashlight before Calla moved it, lay in the corner against a bale of straw with five kittens nursing her. He stood there, watching Calla, sucking on his peppermint and wishing she'd been the one to pop it in his mouth as she had for the horses.

"Hey, babies," she cooed, kneeling to pet them. She glanced over her shoulder at him. "Want to pet them?"

There was so much heart shining in her eyes, all he could do was stare, fascinated, for a beat, then he said, "Sure."

Dane knelt, pulled one glove off and stroked the fluffy coat of one of the tiny kittens. When had he last petted a kitten?

And why the hell was he finding her Norman Rockwell world so appealing? He was definitely a fish out of water here, and he couldn't remember thinking twice about it when he'd come to her farm six months ago.

Maybe it was partly seeing the farm with Calla, spending time in the old farmhouse. His sense of perspective was certainly in a different place than it had been six months ago.

Calla put food in the cat dish and he followed her out of the stall. He pulled his glove back on.

"I owe you an apology," he said.

Her expression showed surprise in the shadows of the old barn. "Why?"

"I shouldn't have said that about you hiding up here. You have a nice life, Calla. You're lucky. The farm, the animals, family and friends nearby, work you clearly enjoy."

"Maybe you have a nice life, too," she said quietly, and he heard the compassion in her voice. Compassion. For him.

He was afraid what he was feeling for her showed on his face, too. Longing, desire.

"Don't we have some shoveling to do?" he asked.

"Sure you're up to it?"

"Sure as I'm going to get."

The horses got watered, then shovels in hand, they were out on the driveway. It was a damn long driveway.

"Are you serious about this?" he asked.

"Yes. Are you backing out? Because I'm doing it with you or without you. I'm hoping for business tonight. I need to clear this snow so people can get up here."

"I'm not backing out."

Dane could think of things he'd rather be doing with her. Like toasting in front of the fire and getting something heartier to eat than the fruit they'd consumed for breakfast.

But anything better than spending the day with Calla doing *anything*, he couldn't imagine. Even if it meant shoveling snow. So, okay.

It took hours. Her dog wandered back up to the house to lounge on the porch. His hands went numb inside the heavy gloves, as did his feet inside the sturdy work boots. The plow, bless it, came by around midmorning, boosting their energy. It was a bonding exercise, he promised himself. And maybe a good reminder that country life wasn't quite that idyllic.

Still, by the time they plopped down on the

still-snowy but well-enough-shoveled driveway three hours later, he felt great. His ribs hurt a bit, but they weren't screaming in agony. He was getting his strength back.

And Calla looked absolutely gorgeous, her face pink, her eyes bright. He couldn't bring himself to look away. He could look at her forever. The house and the barn seemed far away, as did any thought that this incredibly alive woman beside him might die.

The sky was cloudy but the snow had stopped, and what snow covered the ground seemed to reflect what light there was. She wore a red scarf around her neck, tucked in the red jacket she wore, and with the auburn lights in the hair escaping her black wool cap; he would have thought that might clash, but instead it seemed to pick up the red in her hair, accentuate it. The amber flecks in her liquid brown eyes seemed brighter than ever.

Dane wanted to kiss her. He wanted to take her back to the house, and kiss her senseless. Then he'd take her into his arms and make the slowest love ever in front of the fire on that mattress. He longed to see her eyes flaring in desire when he touched her naked body, hear her soft, sexy whimpers when he ran his hands down over her ribs and her belly and lower until she writhed under him. And he yearned to fill every aching need inside her.

The worst part was that he was pretty sure the feeling was mutual. She was attracted to him. But she was scared, too, for some reason. And no way, no how, was he going to live up to her perception of men.

"Thank you," she said, leaning over to wrap her arms around her knees as they sat. "That was a lot of work, but it went twice as fast with help." She cocked her head slightly, studying him. "You *are* an awfully nice man."

He resisted laughing at the irony of that statement considering the very vivid fantasy that had just been running through his mind.

"I'm not that nice. I like you, Calla. Thank you for letting me help you and spend time with you. It's my pleasure."

She shook her head. "You're thanking me after you did all this work? You could have gotten snowbound with someone better prepared, you know. Like, oh, someone who made sure their generator was in good condition in December. Someone who'd taken the neighbor's advice about that tree being sick and how it ought to be cut down before it landed on the house."

"I couldn't imagine anyone I'd rather be snowbound with," he said. "I don't have any complaints. Why do you feel as if you need to apologize for not being perfect, Calla?"

She chewed her lip, looked away. "Like I said, you're a very nice man." She turned her full eyes back to him, and there was something new in them now, something he might have missed if he hadn't been this close to her. A bit of trust. Maybe he'd earned it, but he couldn't imagine ever deserving it. "You don't seem quite real, you know?" she went on softly. "The way you just landed here, practically on my doorstep. And you're so nice, and you tell me I'm pretty, and I keep wondering, if it's all a magical dream, maybe it would actually be okay if—"

His pulse kicked. "If what?"

"If—"

He didn't know what she would have said. The shot came out of nowhere, cracking past his ear.

Chapter 10

Calla screamed, dove to the left, gained her feet and scrambled blindly up the driveway, tripping on the still-slick paving. She fell heavily to her side and hip. Terror thumped through her veins. She was sure her skull would be shattered apart by a bullet any second. Chuck raced down the driveway, barking madly as he reached her.

Arms enfolded her, dragging her back to her feet. J.D.'s arms.

"Don't stop!" He forced her into a dead sprint uphill, holding her by the hand. They reached the house and he shoved her inside ahead of him.

Shock hit her and she sagged against the wall just inside the door. J.D. slammed the door shut after Chuck, who then whined and scratched at the door as if he wanted to run back out and kill someone for her.

"Stay away from the windows." His jaw was granite, his eyes like the ice covering the tree branches outside.

"Oh, my God. We could have been hit. One of us could have been killed." She could hardly feel her feet, her arms. She could barely think. She stood there, shivering, struggling to catch her breath. "You *weren't* hit, were you?" The thought had the breath backing up in her lungs. Instinctively, she reached for J.D., ran her hands worriedly over the jacket, his shoulders, his arms, his chest.

"I wasn't hit," he said.

Relief washed over her, followed by a hot course of anger. "Hunters."

"What do you mean?"

"Must have been hunters. There was a boy killed last year in the next county by a hunter. Lost track of where he was in the woods. Hit the boy while he was playing right outside his own house."

J.D.'s fierce expression didn't change. His tough body looked stiff, restless. He peered out the window then turned back to her.

"We don't know that shot came from a hunter." His voice was calm, controlled. The chill in his eyes frightened her.

She shook her head, his words seeming irrational to her. "What else would it be?"

"Do you have any enemies, Calla?

She blinked. "What?"

"Enemies. People who want you dead."

"No!" She drew in a shuddering breath. "Are you crazy? Of course I don't have enemies. Why would anyone want to kill me?"

"I don't know. That's why I'm asking."

His gaze remained hard and furious. Not angry with her, but angry for her? The silence felt deafening. Outside, she could see nothing but snow and trees. Inside, the front room of the farmhouse was in its newly trashed state from the tree careening down through the roof.

"Well, there's no reason anyone would want to kill me," she said. She had to be the voice of reason here. It had been terrifying. Bone-deep terrifying. But it had been a stupid hunter, not a stalking killer. It was her life. She should know if someone wanted her dead.

His gaze cut to hers, held. Tension whipped the air between them.

"That you know of," he said quietly.

"Okay, stop it," she said. "You're freaking me out."

He didn't look the least bit apologetic about it, either.

"We need to make a police report," he said.

She swallowed hard. "Yes. Of course." She wrestled against backing up, somehow still unnerved by the ferocity of his expression, not to mention the very closeness of him. What had she been about to say out there?

If that shot hadn't scared the hell out of her—

She'd been about to admit that if this really was some big ol' fantasy, they might as well kiss. Maybe more than kiss.

What was a fantasy for if not to be utilized to its full potential?

That shot had been some kind of sign from the universe that kissing J.D. was not part of the fantasy. The fantasy was supposed to stay tucked safe and sound in her head, not practiced full-blown in reality.

"Let's go to the truck," she said. "There haven't been any more shots." Not that she felt overly safe stepping outside again. But up here, away from the road, they were much safer. "I've got No Hunting, No Trespassing signs posted all around the farm. That land across the road is owned by some out-of-staters who rarely come around. They do have a hunting cabin on it. We can have someone from the sheriff's office drive out there and talk to them."

She headed for the phone, gave it a try. The line was still dead. She went to the door. J.D.'s hand slammed down over hers as she touched the knob.

"We're up on a rise here," she pointed out. "Anyone hunting across the road wouldn't be aiming up. You don't aim up to hit a deer." They were vulnerable to that type of accident down there by the road, that's all. And it *had* to have been a stray bullet from a careless hunter. It was a miracle they hadn't been hit, but they should be safe walking to the garage where she kept the truck.

J.D. didn't move his hand. "I'll get the truck, pull it up in front of the house then you come out. Get me the keys."

"That's just stupid."

He lifted a brow. "I'm okay with that."

Her breath backed up in her throat again. She saw more than anger in his deep eyes now. She saw helplessness. As absolutely competent as he was, if that bullet had been an inch to the right, she'd be dead right now and he wouldn't have been able to do a thing about it. And that made him sick, she could see that. Thinking of how she could be dead now didn't feel real good to her, either.

"I don't see why it's okay for you to walk to the garage and not me," she pointed out. "You don't have some invisible supershield. If someone's out there waiting to shoot, you're as vulnerable as me."

"I'm a guy," he said. "Let me be macho. Just this once. It wasn't me who was nearly hit. It was you."

"I don't like macho."

"Noted."

She rolled her eyes, but couldn't deny that he was still scaring her a little. He waited while she got her purse and the keys to the truck.

"Here. You don't have a driver's license, you know."

"Don't care," he said.

He took the keys and headed out. A few minutes later, she watched him pull the old yellow pickup in front of the porch. She ran out and climbed in, slammed the heavy door shut after her.

"See?" she said. "No bullets. And you got to be macho. Happy now?"

He didn't pay any attention to her smart-ass tone, just concentrated on taking the truck cautiously down the slick driveway. She could see the keen way he scrutinized the woods across the road as they hit the highway and she directed him to go right. He accelerated slowly as they pulled away from the farm, driving as fast as road conditions allowed.

Calm. He oozed total calm even as he seemed utterly focused and intense. It made her wonder what he did in real life. The real life he had somewhere out there.

At the sheriff's office, after they reported the shot, they'd explain about the accident, his amnesia. They'd probably take his prints, see if they could match them up, start working to uncover his identity.

Her stomach dropped. What if J.D. didn't come back to the farm with her this afternoon? For all she knew, uncovering his ID might be easy, quick. He could, poof, be out of her life, this oh-so-nice, oh-so-sexy man with the low, rough voice and the knowing eyes and cool intensity that made her feel ridiculously safe. Made her feel as if she could actually trust him, trust a man. For once.

Calla told herself it didn't matter if he came home with her or not. It would be for the best if he didn't. He had some whole other life, away from Haven. She would be an idiot to start getting attached to him.

Her heart panged.

She was already an idiot.

* * *

The sense of tight community hit Dane as they passed the city limit sign for Haven. He had reason, and plenty, to despise Haven. And despise Haven he had, every second he'd sat in jail. But now this was Calla's Haven and the Haven that had cared so much for her life, and her death, and he couldn't help seeing it a little differently now that he knew her.

The town, nestled in thick woods full of oak and hickory and walnut, broken by the sloped pastures and quaint farmhouses of the Appalachian mountains, consisted of little more than a restored town square with a beautiful courthouse. Antique-style lampposts, draped with Christmas pine swags and bright red bows, stood like merry sentinels along the cobbled sidewalks lined with businesses—a dress shop, a clock repair shop, lawyer offices, a craft and consignment retailer and a diner called Almost Heaven. Calla's family's restaurant?

A few side streets held a mix of Victorian-era homes, all decked in holiday style. Another set of side streets held more modern brick businesses. A sign indicated a school up another road. In front of the burger joint, a sign cheered, Go Haven High Honeybees Basketball! The community center advertised a Christmas Eve dinner to raise money for the elevator fund at a local church.

It was still the Haven that had convicted him of a murder he didn't commit. But if he deserved a second chance, maybe Haven did, too.

Calla directed him to the small building behind the courthouse that housed the sheriff's office. Memory washed over Dane's mind of the first time he'd been ushered into this building, and the surreal quality of his life now rushed him. There were entire moments, even hours, when he almost could forget that he was out of place, out of time. Like this morning, with Calla. Before that gunshot.

She was so sure there was nothing suspicious about it. A hunter's screwup. Nothing more. He had no idea how to convince her otherwise, not without telling her a story that would make her scared—but not of a killer, of him. She'd think he was insane. Hell, if it had been him in her shoes, he'd think he was crazy, too.

He could hardly explain the root of his concern to the authorities, either. All he could do was remain alert and at Calla's side. Nonstop.

"Are you ready?"

He shook himself, looked at Calla beside him in the truck. Realized she was waiting for him to pull the keys out of the vehicle and get out.

"Sure."

She reached out unexpectedly and put her hand on his arm, lightly. "Are you nervous? They might be able to help you. Maybe you're about to find out who you are."

He had been so focused on Calla's danger that he hadn't even thought about it. Of course. She'd want to report his accident, the amnesia. He couldn't think of any reason his fingerprints would be on file with law enforcement. Not yet, anyway. Or any reason anyone in the town of Haven would recognize him.

"That's not what I was thinking about," he said honestly.

He saw concern in her eyes, but also a hesitancy he couldn't quite put his finger on.

"I know. You were thinking about me." She withdrew her hand, bit her lip and looked away then. Something was bothering her, and he still wondered what she might have said before that gunshot stopped her. "Come on." She pushed open her door. "Let's go in."

A deputy named Showalter took their statement. He was young, maybe twenty-five, fresh-faced but serious. He nodded, listened, went away for a few minutes and came back with a printout showing the name and out-of-state phone number of the property owners, and agreed to drive out to the cabin himself to check on things, whether or not he got hold of the owners.

Dane resisted the urge to leap across the desk, grab him by the collar and order him to place round-the-clock police protection on Calla's farm. Or maybe he wanted to grab the deputy by the throat because he was the one who had arrested Dane.

"We've been pretty busy dealing with the aftermath of the storm," the deputy said. "But I'll be out there by tonight and if anyone's using the cabin, I'll talk to them. Unless they confess to the accident, we can't pin anything on them, you know. We can't prove it was them unless we can find a bullet on your property that matches up to something they've got, and I promise I'll stop by and look. You might want to look around yourself and see if you find anything. Chances are, you won't. Bullet went past you, thank God, and could have ended up anywhere in the woods off your driveway. Be like looking for a needle in a haystack. Just be glad you didn't get hit."

"What if it wasn't an accident?" Dane pointed out.

The deputy leveled a steady gaze on him. "Be careful is all I can say," he said. "Miss Jones says she doesn't know anyone who'd want to kill her. We don't have anything to go on here. If you think of anything," he added, shooting his gaze back to Calla, "give me a call. Leave a message if I'm not at my desk. You understand," he said, turning back to Dane, "that we have this type of accident more often than we like. Most likely, whoever was responsible heard Miss Jones scream, knew what they did, and they're shaking in their boots somewhere, glad it wasn't worse. You probably won't have any more trouble."

He wasn't making Dane feel particularly better.

"Now, about your accident," Deputy Showalter continued. Calla had briefly explained Dane's predicament when they first arrived. "Let's take prints, start there."

The prints took minutes to make. As Dane wiped the ink from his fingers, he listened to the deputy describe the process. He would call them if their computer turned up any information.

"No accidents have been reported up that way," the deputy said. "No accidents with missing passengers at all that we know about. Of course, we don't know how far you might have walked before you collapsed in front of the farm there." He went over several possibilities, and seemed genuinely intrigued by Dane's mystery.

Calla produced the dry cleaner's receipt. Like the shooting incident, there wasn't much to go on.

"Technically," he explained, "this isn't a police matter. We'll help as much as we can with local social services if you need assistance with shelter, clothing and food. Probably, you could get someone at the paper to do a story. That might be your best bet, especially if you could get the Charleston paper to pick it up. Do you need a referral to social services?"

"I'll make sure he's taken care of," Calla said quickly. She bit her lip, blushed, and her suddenly shy gaze connected with Dane's. "I mean, if that's what you want. I'm fine with you staying at the farmhouse a few more days." She shrugged. "I mean, I could use the help, if you don't mind. But whatever you—"

"Thank you."

Totally embarrassed. That's what she was. Cute, she was that, too. She wanted him to stay with her at the farm.

What Dane really wanted to know was why— because she needed the help, because she had reason to be scared that someone really was trying to kill her and wasn't telling him, or she just wanted…him. And was still fighting it.

Whatever it was, he was damn sure going to find out.

Chapter 11

"I really can't tell much from this receipt. It's torn over the date."

The clerk at A-Plus scrutinized the receipt under the fluorescent light of the dry cleaner's, trying in vain to put the fragmented halves together. Calla watched her, not sure if she was wishing for information or not. J.D. stood beside her at the front counter, close enough to smell his delicious male scent, to feel his body heat even though he wasn't touching her.

"The receipt had gotten wet," she explained to the clerk. "Actually I was wondering if you could look at the number in your record book and see when that might have been." It would at least give J.D. some information about when he'd been in Haven. A clue, maybe.

She was being helpful against her will. It was the right thing to do. Giving in to fantasy—wrong thing to do. Not safe. Or smart.

The clerk looked at the receipt number then shot a blank stare up at Calla.

"This can't be right," she said. She reached over to the receipt book by the cash register, pulled it over and flipped it around to show Calla and J.D. "That number's too high. We're not up to that number in our book."

For a second, Calla couldn't hear anything but the blood rushing through her veins. She looked up at J.D. The expression on his face was unreadable.

"Uh, that can't be right," she agreed.

"No, it can't," the clerk repeated. She reached under the counter and pulled a box out, dug through it. "See?" She brought out another record book, not yet used. "That number is hundreds ahead of where we are now." She flipped through the book. "That receipt is still in our book." She shoved the book, open to the receipt numbered exactly the same as the used and torn receipt Calla had produced.

"But it says A-Plus Cleaners, Haven, WV."
Calla's throat felt tight. "I don't get it."

The clerk shook her head. "It must be an error.
A receipt with a duplicate number that appeared
somewhere earlier in the books. That's all I can
think."

J.D. hadn't spoken. Calla looked at him again.

"Thank you for checking," he said. "I'm sorry
to have bothered you." She felt his fingers trace
her spine then. "It's okay," he told her quietly.
"Come on. Let's go."

Outside the store, they stood on the snowy
walk. The air was crisp, cold, and with all the
decorations, the town square looked like a Christmas card.

"That was weird," Calla said. Very weird. And
disappointing. *Or not.* What now? "Would you
like some lunch? Some hot lunch rather than what
I could do back at the farmhouse?"

J.D. shook his head. "I don't have any money."

Calla made a disgusted snort. "You agreed to
come help out at the farm. Consider it pay. Deal?"

"I'm working for you now?"

"Yeah." She liked that idea. "It's lunchtime.
And I've got work for you to do when we get
back, so don't think you're not going to earn it.
After lunch, we can stop over at the hardware

store and pick up a couple of big tarps to put over the hole in the roof. I can't leave that open like it is."

"Right. Okay, boss lady."

Calla grinned, a buzz of pleasure and excitement knocking back the uneasiness brought on by the oddity of the receipt book at the cleaner's. They walked together along the sidewalk. She thought of how good it might feel to put her gloved fingers between his, to walk hand-in-hand. Light traffic moved on the square, the town still not quite back to normal after the storm.

"Almost Heaven was my parents' family diner," she said. "They owned it together with an uncle, and it's one of my cousins who runs it now. I thought of keeping my share, but at the time my parents died, I was committed to my career with Ledger Pharmaceuticals and I ended up deciding to sell my half to my cousin."

"Ever regret that?"

She shrugged. "Not really. It's still in the family, and I'm glad of that. I'm content with the farm."

Content? The word struck her. Mostly, though, J.D. had made her start to wonder if she'd been missing out on more than she'd realized.

An old, familiar tug of nerves hit her gut. No

matter what she knew was smart, she was letting herself fall for this stranger. What did she really know about him? Nothing. Hadn't she learned her lesson about being stupid with men? About trusting too much, too soon?

They reached the door of the diner and J.D. reached for the handle just as a customer came out. The man stopped short, as did Calla's pulse.

Lovely timing. Her lesson, in the flesh. The worst thing about coming back to her hometown was seeing her old nightmare walking around on the streets. It didn't happen often, but it was always too often for her liking. Usually she was able to avoid actual conversation.

This was not her lucky day.

"Hey, babe," he said. "Nice to see you."

She hated that. Babe. Baby girl. Sweetie. Dear. She hated the endearments that never sounded like endearments to her. Not when they'd too often been followed by cruel words. His close-cropped dark blond hair and chiseled features made Brian Reilly good-looking to most women, but Calla saw past it. Had since about three days after they'd married. Three days too late. His gray eyes looked cold to her now, his powerful build menacing, his perfect features fake, his charm nothing but lies.

"Hi, Brian," she responded as briefly as possible.

"Friend of yours?" Brian inquired, sizing up J.D. rather noticeably.

"J.D. We were just going in to eat. Nice to see you, too." Not nice at all, but she hoped he'd take the hint and get out of their way.

"I'm Brian Reilly." He stuck his hand out, introducing himself despite Calla's obvious and intentional lapse in offering to do so. "Are you new here? I don't recall seeing you around."

"Somewhat," J.D. said.

"Did you get those pictures I sent?" Brian asked, returning his attention to Calla.

"Yes. Thanks." There weren't many people who made her feel scared and small anymore, but Brian did.

J.D. made her feel secure and equal. She liked that. Even when he was playing the macho card, she hadn't felt like she was being demeaned. She'd felt protected.

She made a vain attempt to move past him, but he wouldn't budge.

"I'd like to talk to you sometime, Calla."

"I'm busy," she said tensely. "I'm busy right now, actually, so if you don't mind—"

J.D. put his hand on her spine again. She could feel, even through her jacket, both the tension of him as well as the support if she needed it.

"I need to talk to you," Brian repeated.

As usual, Brian's needs came ahead of anyone else's. Especially hers.

"I don't need to talk to you," she bit out. "Please—"

"The lady would like to go inside," J.D. said calmly, but the steel in his voice told her he meant business.

She swallowed tightly. She didn't want things to get ugly on the street.

"What do you want?" she asked Brian. "It's cold, you know."

"We can go inside," Brian suggested. "It won't take long, but I'd like to talk to you alone. You never answer the phone if I call, and you know I can't come out to the farm."

She'd had a restraining order against him at one time, though it was no longer in place. She figured he thought she'd call the police, though, if he showed up. She might.

"Whatever you want to say, say it now," she said. "And fast. Okay? I really am cold."

He sighed, and the sound annoyed her. "Okay, have it your way, Calla. Look, I've got a new job, that's all. I've quit drinking and I'm going to counseling."

"Good for you." Maybe he'd stick with it this

time, maybe not. It wasn't her problem and it didn't matter, and mostly she hated that his voice still sent shivers up her spine.

"It's part of my counseling to apologize to everyone I've hurt. I want to apologize to you, Calla."

"Good. Thanks."

"I'm sorry."

"Okay." He was done, right? She wasn't sure in that moment what was worse—the way just seeing him brought bad memories back, or the overwhelming embarrassment of J.D. witnessing this little scene.

"I'd still like to talk to you alone," he persisted.

"No."

"I think this conversation is over," J.D. put in. "The lady's cold, and we're hungry. So if you don't mind…"

Calla realized her legs were trembling. Stupid. She wanted to put the weakness down to the freezing temps, but she knew it wasn't the weather that was to blame.

She was relieved when Brian stepped aside. The diner was warm and noisy, half the tables and booths filled with a good lunch crowd. The diner was a hundred years old and had been through a few renovations, but it retained the antiquey charm with original metal-legged stools at the soda fountain counter, and linoleum tabletops in shiny red that contrasted nicely against the black and white tiled walls. Photographs of celebrities, mostly minor, hung on the walls, all autographed, and the original oak floor slanted just enough to make it quaint.

They seated themselves, and Shelly, one of the waitresses, came over, said a cheerful hello to Calla, looked the stranger over with a slightly lustful curiosity that normally would have amused Calla, and then recited the day's specials.

"I'll tell Meg you're here," Shelly said. "I know she'll want to pop over if she gets a minute. Now, what can I get for you?"

She ordered a cheeseburger and onion rings, and J.D. asked for a fried bologna sandwich and fries.

"Meg's my cousin," she said after the waitress left, filling the silence that seemed to weigh heavy even as chatter and the clink of flatware and dishes rang around them.

"I wasn't wondering who Meg was," J.D. said quietly.

She finally turned her gaze to his. "I know." She sighed. "Thanks for your help."

"You didn't need it, but I'm glad I was there."

She frowned. "I needed the help," she said. "I'd still be out there if it weren't for you."

"You did fine. You were polite, and calm."

She wasn't sure what to say to that. She hadn't felt calm. And she hadn't been thinking polite things.

"I didn't take his apology very well."

"He hurt you."

She felt a pang in her chest. "Yeah." She wrapped her arms across her chest and leaned into the edge of the table, stared at the wall, noticed the fine cracks in the grout between the tiles.

"Want to talk about it?"

"No."

"Okay."

"He's my ex-husband," she said abruptly, looking back across the table. "I was young and not so smart. I got pregnant and I married him. He hit me so hard one day that I fell down the steps behind our apartment and I lost the baby. I was still young and still not so smart. I stayed with him for another six months before I got up the guts to divorce him and then I went to West Virginia University, did my undergrad and postgrad, then went to work for Ledger Pharmaceuticals at the research facility. I came back to Haven after my grandfather died. Life story." She spit it all out in a rush. Apparently she wanted to talk about it after all.

"I think you might have left some details out."

"That's okay." She'd said enough. Maybe too much.

She forced herself to meet his gaze that glittered with anger, and a million other things she couldn't deal with. For just a minute, a very weak minute, she wanted to cry. If he said something like he was sorry, she *would* cry. She hated it when people said they were sorry, which was one good reason she rarely told anyone her life story, even the abbreviated version.

"I'm sorry," he said.

Surprisingly his statement made her mad instead of making her cry. "Don't say that!" Dammit, she hadn't expected it from him. "I hate it when people act like they are sorry for me."

"I'm not sorry for you," he said calmly. "I'm sorry I didn't knock him on his ass when I had the chance."

Right there, right then, when she was still trembling, still upset over the confrontation with Brian, she started laughing. "You're so sweet," she managed to say, struggling to get a straight face back.

J.D. shot her a wide, wonderful, heart-stopping smile. "Not really," he said. "But it's okay with me if you think so."

Their food came, and so did Meg, who plopped

down long enough to get the whole story—about J.D., about the roof, about the gunshot. She was a year older than Calla, and a friend as much as a cousin.

Meg fussed. "I'm so glad you weren't hit. I'm glad you reported it, too. But, I gotta say, your luck's not all bad." She eyed J.D., and a flush waved across Calla's face. "Your nonpracticing lesbian days might be over."

"Excuse me?" J.D. looked confused.

"Nothing," Calla said, eyeing Meg sternly.

"She can explain later," Meg said airily. She tugged on Calla's arm as she scooted out of the booth. "Come on. I've got to get back to the kitchen and I've got something to give you."

Calla followed her to the office in the back of the diner. Meg shut the door of the cramped room.

"Wow," Meg said.

Calla rolled her eyes even as her stomach tightened. She knew what Meg was thinking. Meg was single, and she was definitely no lesbian, nonpracticing or otherwise.

"Okay, if you've got something to give me, give it to me so I can get going," Calla said, attempting to cut to the chase. "I love you but I've got stuff to do."

"He is so damn hot, that's all I've got to say,"

Meg said. She sat behind her desk and rummaged in an overfull drawer. "Really hot. And wow, do you see how he looks at you?" she went on, proving she did, indeed, have much more to say.

"He's nice," Calla said. "And patient, really patient. And understanding. Not pushy at all. And helpful, really helpful." Now she was getting carried away, though everything she'd said was true. She didn't want to encourage Meg, though. She was having enough trouble controlling her urge to take him back to the farmhouse and slam him onto that mattress in front of the fire and live out that soap opera fantasy.

"And hot. Don't forget hot."

"I can't! You keep reminding me!" As if she needed reminding.

"Here." Meg had finally found what she was looking for. She came around the desk, shoved something small into Calla's hand and simultaneously pushed her out the door. "I know you'll need them. I gotta get to work. Merry Christmas." She disappeared.

Calla looked down at her hand and found two pretty purple plastic-wrapped condoms.

If Santa didn't stop being so good to her, she was going to have a heart attack.

Chapter 12

Dane smoothed the tarp as he crawled across the roof of Calla's farmhouse, beating back the wind that kicked up and dusted snow in his face. He'd brought several cinder blocks up first and used them to weigh down the extralarge tarp they'd picked up at the hardware store before heading out of town.

Brian Reilly's exchange with Calla lurked at the edge of Dane's thoughts, not to mention what little Calla had told him about their brief marriage. Was Reilly sincere? Or were his words a foreboding sign of some obsession with Calla that could lead to murder?

She hadn't mentioned the stalking ex before. What else hadn't she mentioned? She was starting to open up to him, but it was slow, and that gunshot earlier reminded him that he had no guarantees of when someone might try to kill Calla again. He was reliving the past—but he wasn't reliving the *exact* past. His throwback in time hadn't come with any rules he could count on.

He knew Calla was in the house right now working to clean up the front room as best as possible. Could he steal a moment to take a look inside her office in the barn? He didn't like the idea of sneaking around and poking in Calla's things, but so far nothing was coming together to give him any clear signs. The stalking ex. The supposedly random hunting accident. Her firing from Ledger. The pieces were disparate, and nothing stood out.

After that gunshot, he didn't even like the idea of Calla walking outside her house. He'd squashed her suggestion of walking down to the road to look for the bullet in the woods. It was a hopeless idea anyway, and it hadn't been hard to convince her it was too dangerous, even if she did believe it had been a hunting accident. But he couldn't hold her prisoner, or explain why he was so sure someone was out to kill her. And unless she opened up, and soon, that left getting information behind her back in any way he could.

He'd spotted a laptop computer in her bedroom. Would he find anything on the computer—letters, files, that might tell him something? He'd been over his own files while he'd sat in prison. He'd been unable to see any connection at Ledger that would explain Calla's murder.

"Hey!"

He looked down as he placed the last cinder block, saw Calla standing out in the wind below, bundled up in her jacket and wool cap. So gorgeous.

"The electricity's back!" she shouted up, grinning wide. "Phone, too."

He gave her the thumbs-up sign. She held the ladder while he climbed down.

"All set up there," he said. "Should hold till you can get someone out here to repair the roof."

"Great. Thanks. I've got the inside cleaned up, or at least passable for human habitation. The heater kicked on, so pretty soon we should be practically living in the modern age again, if you don't mind a one-hundred-year-old farmhouse."

"Don't mind it a bit."

She studied him, her gaze serious and sweet.

His heart gave a treacherous little lurch. He was getting in way too deep here, and he knew it. In her eyes were all the things he felt, too—fear, trepidation, hope.

"I was thinking we'd celebrate a little bit. I'll cook something for dinner later and I was thinking we'd go get a tree. I'll put a tree up. Will you help me pick one out? We'll have to wait till late for dinner if some customers come out, though."

She was going to put a Christmas tree up. It was a little thing, but it seemed big, somehow. Her eyes shone and her cheeks glowed.

"Yes," he said. "I'd love to. Thank you."

"For what?"

"Thank you for letting me be part of your life here."

He could see her swallow, hard.

"J.D." Her eyes looked huge and nervous.

He waited. She didn't say anything more, just stared at him.

"Calla?"

The waiting for her to speak was torture. His stomach was firmly lodged in his throat for some reason.

"I'm scared about you staying here," she said finally, quickly. "I know it was my idea, but I'm scared."

"Why?" He thought they were past that, thought she trusted him more than that now.

"Never mind." She whipped around, made a beeline for the house.

"Wait!" He went after her, grabbed her arm. "What are you scared of, Calla? I'm not going to hurt you. I promise."

She looked so troubled, it made his chest hurt.

"I know you're not," she said in a small voice. "I mean, I know you're not going to hurt me the way you're thinking. Physically."

"I don't want to hurt you in any way, Calla."

"I guess it's not you I'm scared of. It's me."

"What do you mean?"

"I'm scared I'm going to get too attached to you," she burst out, her voice rising. She pulled her arm away from him, backed up a step as if she needed the distance. "Too used to having you around. Then you're going to remember who you are and you'll be gone. You have some whole other life out there you'll want to go back to."

"Maybe. Maybe not." She was afraid of getting too attached to him. She was falling for him. He wasn't sorry—not one damn bit—even if it was a bad idea, for her and for him. "Maybe you'll be stuck with me. Maybe I'll never leave." And why did that sound so good? "I like Haven. I like your farm." Was it possible he could stay in Haven? He kept trying to not let himself even think about the future. He wasn't sure either of them had one. What if they didn't? What if they *really* didn't? Maybe he couldn't stop the hand of fate. She could have been killed this morning. She could be killed anytime. For all he knew, *he* could be killed. And if now was all they had… It wasn't a reason to stay away from Calla. It was a reason to do the complete opposite. Life could turn on a dime; he'd learned that, if nothing else. "I like *you*, Calla."

She searched his face. He could see the panic building in her eyes, still. "You're the nicest man I've ever met."

"Then you haven't met enough men," he joked.

Calla made a choked sound that didn't quite sound like a laugh. He closed the step between them, slowly.

"I've met plenty," she said, and she sounded breathless. She chewed her lip, drawing his attention to her very kissable mouth. "I don't like most of them. I like you." Her wary eyes dropped.

He reached up, tipped her chin so that she met his gaze again.

"Good."

"I don't deserve someone like you," she said suddenly.

"Why would you say that? Calla, what's wrong?"

He realized now that she was blinking back tears, frantically.

"I don't know. I'm being stupid. Just forget I said anything."

Forget? Not likely.

"Calla…" He drew his hand away, then touched her again, just a light skim across her cheek before dropping it back to his side. "Let's go get the tree, okay?"

Slow. She needed slow.

And he might have so little time.

Calla really needed Pete and Jimmy. Thank God she had J.D.

Customers started showing up as they were dragging their tree back to the farmhouse. All it took to be ready for business was to turn on the lights and music in the barn and get the hot water heating for drinks. During the season, she stayed prepared.

Some arrived to cut down trees they'd tagged weeks ago, while others straggled through the snowy field, making their decision. J.D. worked like a trooper, helping to haul the trees back to the barn, load them on trucks or tie them into yawning car trunks, while she manned the register inside.

A couple of twin girls, maybe four, were spilling hot chocolate all over the barn floor when J.D. walked in. One of the girls started crying, looking around for their mother who'd wandered off to look at the wreaths Calla had moved to a table outside the barn.

"Hey." J.D. knelt, talked to the little girl eye to eye. "It's no biggie. There's more. Want a peppermint, too?" He handed her a peppermint and poured another cup of hot water into her cup with another packet of chocolate mix.

"There's kittens in the back of the barn," he said when he gave her the cup. "Want to ask your mom if you can go see them?"

The girls both squealed, the spill forgotten, and ran outside for their mom, hot chocolate sloshing in the cups in their hands.

"You don't mind if they pet the kittens, do you?" he asked Calla.

She shook her head. "No. Of course not. It was sweet of you to think of it."

He grinned. White teeth, big smile, twinkling blue eyes. Adorable. There was heat in his eyes, too. Heat that seemed to arrow straight from him to her. He leaned on the counter near the register, leaned over toward her where she stood behind it.

"You're pretty sweet yourself," he said huskily.

"Don't."

"Don't what?" He looked innocent.

She swallowed hard. "Don't make me like you so much."

He was really good at looking at her as if nothing else in the world existed, even as the mom and two girls came back into the barn.

"The kittens are in the back," she told them. "Past the stall with the Appaloosas."

The mom held each girl by the hand and a few seconds later they could be heard crying "horsies!" and making neighing sounds.

"They're cute," J.D. said.

He was cute.

"I always wanted to have twins," she said, then felt like sticking a sock in her mouth. What'd she have to say that for?

"Looks fun," he said. "One at a time might be easier, though."

"I had these twin dolls," Calla explained. "Maybe it was my only-child thing. I wished I had a brother or sister, mostly a sister. I got twin dolls one year for Christmas and I loved them to death. Carried them everywhere. My mom taught me to sew and I made little outfits for them."

"You'd be a good mom."

Would she? Maybe she'd never find out, the way things were going.

"You don't know that," she said. "You haven't known me very long."

"Long enough," he said slowly. His hand had moved to cover hers. He felt warm, strong. "You don't give yourself enough credit, I know that. And you hold back a lot. I know that, too."

"It's my defense."

"I know that, too."

Damn him. He really did see right through her. The strange thing was, she felt like she knew him, too. Like she'd always known him, which was especially weird since the truth was neither of them even knew his name. It was like they connected, though.

She liked it. And it scared her at the same time.

"You're getting kinda arrogant now," she said, and she sounded breathless to her own ears. He was still staring at her, and it was making her feel crazy. Crazy like she wanted to lean over the counter and kiss him.

Lucky for her, they heard gravel crunching outside and more customers were arriving.

She closed up and locked the register.

"I'm going to go check on them in the back, and you'd better see if those customers who just got here want some help out in the field."

He smiled at her again, that grin of his that

sank heat straight to her marrow. "See ya later, boss."

By the time she stepped outside, she could see him heading out to the field with what looked like a big family. She served up hot chocolate and sold wreaths and a few candles for the next hour and was leaning up against the barn when he came back with another group—grandparents with a couple of boys they'd brought to pick out their tree. It was getting dark, and a few flakes were falling, just floating lightly against the deep twilight sky. The Christmas lights strung along the frame of the barn twinkled.

She was still thinking about kissing him. Thinking hard. It was a big decision, the whole idea of making the first move.

A red Jeep came up the driveway, stopped and shut its lights. J.D. was helping the old man tie the tree into their car trunk.

"Hey, babe."

Calla's nerves froze.

Brian strode toward her. She was aware of J.D.'s gaze yanking around, watching.

She straightened. "I thought you wouldn't come out to the farm," she said.

"I changed my mind. I still need to talk to you alone, Calla."

"*I* don't need to talk to *you* alone," she countered.

J.D. left the old man, the tree not secured in the car yet.

Brian jerked his head around, saw him coming. "Tell your watchdog to back off, Calla."

"I'm not telling him anything," she said. "I'm telling you to leave my property."

J.D. reached them. "You heard the lady. Leave."

The two boys that had come with the older couple came running around the side of the barn, chasing each other. Their laughter carried on the icy air. The grandmother got out of the car and came around the back to help her husband finish securing the tree.

"This is none of your business," Brian ground out.

She could see his hands fisting convulsively at his sides. Yeah, he'd changed. Right.

"Look, I've got customers here," she said desperately.

"Give me five minutes alone," he said. "Five. Then I'll leave. I promise, Calla."

Dammit. She so didn't want trouble.

"I'll give you three," she clipped out. She looked at J.D. "Please," she said, softer. "Give me a couple minutes. I'm not going inside," she told Brian. "You can talk to me out here."

J.D.'s mouth set in a hard line. She could see

the concern in his eyes and the stiff way he held himself. But he did as she asked, backed off enough for them to speak privately, though he didn't take his eyes off her.

"What do you want?" she asked Brian.

"I still love you, Calla."

"What?" God, she hadn't expected that.

"I love you, Calla. Always have. My head's clear now. I don't drink anymore, haven't in months. I miss you."

"We haven't been married in years!" Her head reeled.

"You think that means I don't miss you? There's nobody else for me, Calla. Just you. I'm sorry about everything. I was young and stupid. Hell, we both were. We didn't do it right. I just want another chance."

She shook her head, uneasiness sharpening her spine. "I can't give you one, Brian. That was a long time ago. I'm sorry you feel that way. And I'm glad if you're in counseling and working, and not drinking. But that doesn't change anything about us. That was over a long time ago."

"It doesn't have to be."

"It *is*."

His face changed suddenly, changed to what she realized was a look of disgust.

"It's him, isn't it?" he spat. He closed the foot of space between them and she instinctively retreated, her back hitting the barn. "That guy. You were with him in town today, and now here he is, working on the farm with you. You always were a whore."

"And you always were an ass." She felt cold, cold and scared, but determined, so determined suddenly, that no man, especially Brian, was going to talk to her that way ever again. Maybe she didn't deserve someone as wonderful as J.D., but she didn't deserve Brian or anything he'd ever done to her. "I wouldn't want you if you were the last man on earth. Now get off my property. You had your five minutes."

J.D. moved so fast, she didn't even see him coming till he was there. "Get off the lady's property."

Brian said something, under his breath, and backed up. He gave a last, scathing look at Calla.

"You're stupid, Calla, and you're gonna be sorry. I was the best you ever had, the best you'll ever get. You're stupid and ugly and a whore and you know it."

J.D. took one step and put himself directly between Brian and Calla. "I said, get out of here." Anger hardened his voice to something she barely recognized.

Brian stared back at him for a beat, then turned, strode to his car.

The grandmother was calling to the boys and the older man was giving a last check to the rope securing the tree in the back of his car. Thank God they couldn't have heard what had gone on. Brian's Jeep roared down the driveway.

"That was fun," she said in a voice that she wished could have come out bigger.

J.D. looked at her. "Are you okay?"

She was shaking like a leaf. But yeah, she was okay. Blinking furiously, she said, "Of course." Then she started crying, big hot tears rolling down her cheeks.

J.D. reached up, thumbed them away with his gloved hand, then he folded her into his arms. God, he felt good. "Yeah," he said softly, reaching between them to tip her face up now to meet his eyes, concern still sparking there, "you're okay, Calla. You're more than okay."

He made her feel like she really was. She was still trembling, and suddenly she didn't care, didn't want to think about it. She leaned up, kissed him, just the softest press of her mouth to his, just a tiny, tiny kiss that sent buzzing sensations all over her body that weren't tiny at all.

She smiled into his eyes when she pulled away, saw the amazed look in his dark depths.

"Hi," she said.

He laughed softly. She wanted... Oh, she wanted more than a kiss and she was suddenly impatient about it.

"I think that'll be the last of the business for tonight," she said. "You still up for a nice dinner?"

He nodded. "Oh, yeah."

"I'm going to go thank them before they leave," she said, nodding at the customers. "They're regulars every year. You want to turn the lights off in the barn for me? Meet me back at the house?"

"Okay." He smiled again, and she watched him go inside.

As she stood there thinking, she was barely aware of sound, a roar. And she pulled back, realized a vehicle had barreled back up the driveway. Realized it was Brian.

Realized the boys belonging to the older couple were running back around the barn, toward their grandmother, who'd been calling them. Realized the sound the grandmother was making now was a scream.

Realized Brian had jumped out of the Jeep with a knife.

Chapter 13

Wind kicked up and the Christmas lights strung along the barn glinted off the knife in Brian's hand. The boys had seen the dangerous-looking blade and they'd stopped short, several feet from their grandparents.

Nobody moved.

Oh God. Where was J.D.?

Brian moved so fast, she didn't see more than a blur in her panicked state. Her pulse hammered. He had one of the boys, his arm wrapped around the child's chest, straddling him against the front of his body. The knife at the boy's throat.

The grandmother screamed again and her husband reached for her and the other boy at the same time. The second boy ran to his grandparents. The grandfather pushed the boy to his wife, then stepped forward.

"Take me instead," he said roughly, his voice shaking but loud. "I don't know what you want, but don't hurt the boy."

The grandmother started praying.

Brian backed away, dragging the first boy with him. The boy's eyes were wide, dark, terrorized.

Calla stepped forward. "He wants me," she said. Her knees felt like water, but no way was she standing by while that boy got hurt. Brian had lost it—really lost it. She knew he'd been watching her since she'd come back to Haven. Maybe seeing her in town with J.D. had made him crack. Who knew what else was going on in his life these days? He'd never been emotionally healthy. "Just let the boy go, Brian. Let him go, and get back in your car and drive away. It's the right thing to do. You know it."

"The right thing is for us to be together, Calla. I waited, for years, and you came back to Haven, just like I always knew you would. You came back because you couldn't stay away from me."

"I didn't come back because of you, Brian."

The boy made a noise and his grip tightened. She could only stare at the vicious flash of metal. *Please, please, don't let him hurt the boy....*

She saw something move in the shadows. There was someone in the woods. Her heart pumped wildly. J.D.!

He moved silently. He must have heard what was happening from the barn, slipped around the back—

She had to get the boy away from that knife, distract Brian enough that J.D. could do something, help them.

"Just let the boy go," she said, taking another careful step toward Brian and the boy. "Please. I'll do whatever you want."

"Please," Brian mimicked. "Sure, now you beg. I always did have to show who was boss, didn't I, Calla?"

"Yes, you're the boss, Brian."

She kept coming at him, one slow step at a time.

"You're coming with me, Calla. We'll blow this town. Leave everything behind. Just you and me. It's what we should have done a long time ago. I'm sick of all these people you have around you all the time. Soon as I get rid of one, you get another."

"What are you talking about?"

"I can do anything I want, Calla. It's useless to try to stop me, you know. I got rid of Pete and Jimmy, didn't I?"

Her throat closed up. "What?" she asked thinly.

"Me and Pete, we know how that works. Once an alcoholic, always an alcoholic. Jimmy was a little more trouble."

What was he saying? Calla's head reeled.

"I've been watching you," Brian said. "I scared Jimmy off. Told him there was a bear out there, told him it attacked me. Told him I saw it on your farm. He freaked. Pete, I just told him to beat it or I'd kill him with my bare hands."

She went cold inside, absolutely cold. "Did you shoot at me from the woods today?" She'd stopped two feet away from him.

J.D. stood silent, waiting, just behind him. The grandparents had seen him and she heard the woman's breath catch at her question.

"So what if I did?" Brian asked, and laughed. God, he laughed. "I guess I didn't scare your new friend off. Where is your friend?"

His body went even more rigid. If he turned, if he saw J.D.— Dozens of scenarios rolled through her head, but it was the thought of the boy, what might happen to the boy, that spurred her to action.

Brian's head turned, slowly, almost as if in slow motion. Calla knew it was now or never. She closed the gap, grabbed the boy's arm, shoved him toward his grandparents even as Brian whipped back around, fumbling to grab her.

J.D. lunged at him, tackling him to the ground. The knife went flying as Calla fell, rolled out of the way of the two men, stretched for the knife, scrambling to her feet.

Sirens sounded in the distance. J.D. must have called 911 from the barn before he'd come outside. He had Brian down, was sitting on top of him, his powerful hands pinning her ex-husband's arms to either side of his head while Brian spewed profanities and threats.

The old man leaped into action, grabbed more of the heavy twine from the huge roll that was used for securing trees for transport, cut off a piece and ran to J.D., knelt behind Brian, tied his wrists over his head by the time the state trooper car rolled up, and helped J.D. hold him down till the troopers got out.

Calla shivered. The danger was past, but the thought of what might have happened hit her, really hit her, and she almost fell to her knees. Her muscles shook violently.

Then J.D. was there, his arms around her.

"It was Brian," she whispered shakily, staring at him, searching his face. "It wasn't a hunter. It was Brian. He ran off Pete and Jimmy. He was— He wanted to kidnap me." God, what would have happened then? What if she had been alone when Brian had snapped?

"He's not going to do anything, not ever again," J.D. said. "He's going to jail, and thank God there are plenty of witnesses."

"Thank God there was you," she said tightly, tears welling, threatening to spill over. She continued to shake. Shock. She was in shock, she realized in a numb, distant way.

"I'm here," he told her softly, holding her against him. "I'm here and I'm not going anywhere."

Dane studied Calla's face. Was that it? Was the danger over? The image of Brian Reilly grabbing for Calla with that knife still in his hand… It was going to haunt him forever. And it made no sense to him. Had he sent Brian Reilly over the edge by staying with Calla, by going into town with her today? There had been no evidence during the trial about Calla's ex-husband. The ex-husband hadn't even been mentioned. He might as well not have existed as far as Dane had known. There had been not one iota of suspicion attached to him.

Was this just another way the past had been changed by his presence in Calla's home, or had Brian been her killer?

Was it over? A desperate hope flickered inside him. He wanted the danger to be over. He wanted Calla to be safe.

And yet he couldn't shake the dreadful feeling that she wasn't, that this wasn't the end of it.

The Christmas tree was butt ugly. It was the ugliest tree on the farm. And that was exactly why she'd picked it. Calla couldn't stand to take a tree out for personal use that she could sell.

But for some reason, she loved it anyway. And right then, for the first time in a long time, she loved Christmas. Not for other people, but for herself.

The troopers had finally finished taking everyone's statements, and they'd driven off with Brian in the back of the patrol car. Two hours later, the whole thing seemed surreal. Even now, she couldn't believe it had happened.

"Merry Christmas, Charlie Brown," she said, smiling up at J.D. Jeez, he looked good. The fragrance of pine and the sweet smell of the homemade elderberry wine she'd taken out of the cellar and served in crystal goblets that hadn't seen the light of day in who knows how long mixed with the sexy man scent of her stranger.

Her stranger. That's how she thought of him. Hers. All hers. Maybe she'd had too much wine already. But then, she deserved it tonight, didn't she? After what had happened with Brian.

Why had J.D. shown up at her farm? She was way too old to believe in Santa. Did she believe in destiny? Was he supposed to be here?

Or was she just trying to convince herself it would be okay if she used what Meg had given her?

She dragged a strand of garland out of the box of Christmas decorations she'd brought out from the cellar along with the wine. The scrawny, lopsided tree was looking better already.

The kitchen timer dinged at the same time the phone rang.

She jumped for it. They'd put the tree up in the kitchen, in the corner where the antique high chair had been. She'd moved it temporarily to the cellar. For now, the front room might be passably cleaned up and sealed from the elements, but there was still a hunk of tree in it that would need a chainsaw, and another day, to get out. They'd moved the mattress back to the bedroom. With the power back, the house should be toasty-warm all over by bedtime.

"This is Deputy Showalter."

"Oh. Hi."

"Just wanted to touch base with you. I know about the incident up at your place tonight, and we're pretty sure it was your ex-husband who did that shooting as well. I got hold of the Boatwrights. They're in New Hampshire. They do have some friends using the place this week, and I was able to find them when I drove by the cabin earlier. They said they hadn't even been hunting today, but that's not surprising. I didn't find any sign of a bullet when I stopped by your place to check around down there along the road. Anyway, the Boatwrights' guests have gotten a warning and hopefully things will be fine if it was them, but right now it's looking like we can put this down to Brian Reilly. If there's any more trouble, give us a call."

"Thank you."

"Be careful out there." The deputy hung up.

"That was the deputy," she told J.D., and explained what he'd had to say.

"I'd feel better if they found a gun on Brian and were able to do some ballistics, prove it."

"Come on," she said. "Don't worry so much."

"I just want you to be safe, Calla."

"I'm safe right now." Was she? She wasn't

thinking safe thoughts. She was thinking about wild, hot, raw animal sex with her stranger.

He'd taken a shower when he'd come inside, and she'd followed up with one of her own while he'd gotten started decorating without her. Then she'd gotten the wine and started thinking about how deliciously, dangerously good he looked.

And about the condoms burning a hole in her pocket. Yes, she had put them in her *pocket*. Like she needed to be *prepared*.

Scary.

And all she could think about was how badly she wanted to take them *out* of her pocket.

"We'd better eat," she said. Food. To counteract the effects of the inhibition-reducing homemade wine. Good plan.

And well, really. He had said he liked her. He had said he noticed her. He had said, wow. But did he even *want* her? Want her in bed? He hadn't tried a thing. Not that she wanted him to turn into an animal, but that's what men did. They weren't shy about asking, even demanding, what they wanted. She was the one who'd kissed him, not the other way around.

"It smells incredible," he said. "Whatever it is."

She'd thrown things together while he'd been in the shower. "It's just chicken. Easy chicken.

Throw in a can of tomatoes and some rice. Cook for an hour. No biggie." She'd popped open a can of green beans and heated up some leftover corn bread.

If he'd moved toward her, just the slightest, she was sure she would just toss the chicken out the window and throw herself at him. Thank God he didn't, thus saving her from that humiliating display of lust. Instead he moved toward the cabinets, got down plates, pulled open a drawer, grabbed silverware while she made a mental list of plausible reasons they could skip dinner and go straight to using Meg's present.

The list was just for her, of course. She didn't intend to share it.

He'd dropped the conversation about her safety, and she knew he sensed she didn't want to discuss it, didn't want to talk about Brian and the awful scene outside the barn. She was grateful to him for that.

"So what was with that nonpracticing lesbian thing?" he asked when they'd sat down with plates heaping with food Calla didn't feel the least bit hungry to eat.

She made a disgusted noise, not sure this topic of conversation was any better than the other one she wanted to avoid. "Don't pay any attention to

Meg. She thinks she's funny." She took a bite of chicken.

"Is that why you don't date? You're a nonpracticing lesbian, whatever that is?"

Calla sighed, put her fork down. "It's just a joke. Means I'm not dating, yes. I'm not a lesbian, but I'm not interested in men, or in men who think they can own women."

"Nobody can own another person."

"That's right." She took another bite. The food was good and she *was* hungry, she remembered. And she'd rather eat than have this conversation.

"I guess it's a good way to put off men, if that's what you're after," he said casually, but the gaze he turned on her when she lifted her eyes was anything but casual. It was intense, interested, like he really wanted to hear what she had to say.

"What do you mean?"

"Lesbian. Just the word scares most men."

She laughed. "I like it because when you throw in the nonpracticing part, no one knows what it means. Men get lost trying to figure it out and forget they were hitting on you. 'You want to go out?' 'I'm sorry. I'm a nonpracticing lesbian.' I've used that line. Works well."

Now he laughed, then his gaze sobered. "You didn't use it on me."

"You didn't hit on me," she pointed out, and the nervous tug in her belly reminded her that this was dangerous territory.

She picked up the glass of wine and downed it.

"Calla?" She was totally not going to look at him. He'd see what she wanted if she did. He'd see that she wanted *him*. Terror washed her. She wanted him. She liked him. He liked her. There was nothing stopping them from doing something about it other than the fact that he didn't seem to want her back, not in that way.

Or if he did, he'd made a decision not to do anything about it, which had the same end result. He wasn't interested in pursuing a relationship with her.

"What?" she asked, staring at her plate.

"Do you want me to hit on you?"

Chapter 14

"No!" Yes. Well, not exactly. Did she? Calla's body tingled in awareness. Here was the sexiest, most attractive man she'd ever known and he was looking at her with smoldering, sparking eyes and asking her if she wanted him to hit on her.

"Okay," he said.

Disappointment soaked her. What had she expected? Other than telling her she was pretty, he hadn't said or done anything to suggest he wanted to pursue anything.

"Because I'm not going to," he went on.

"You don't have to explain." Sheesh. She went back to her food.

"I think I do."

"No, you don't." She looked up from her plate, studied the buttons of his newly donned flannel shirt, avoiding directly looking at his face. "You really don't."

"I don't hit on women. At least," he added quickly, "I don't think I do. I don't think that's my style. That doesn't feel right to me."

"Feel right?"

"Respectful," he explained.

"What?" Now she put her fork down, met his gaze head-on.

With his eyes steady on hers, he repeated what he'd said. "Respectful. Is there something you don't understand about that?"

"Men are usually pretty direct," she said slowly. "They say what they want, and they want what their first-floor brain tells them they want."

"First-floor?"

"You know what I mean."

"I have a brain, Calla, and I don't keep it in my pants. You have a brain, too. I like your brain. I like you. I respect you."

She didn't know what to say, but she knew he

was serious. He meant what he was saying. Then he just smiled at her while her heart somersaulted.

"I think you were trying to tell me something earlier, a couple of times, and I was just thinking it might help you if I told you how I felt about you," he went on. "Maybe it would help you trust me, and get you past whatever is going on in that complicated head of yours, if you knew."

What was he telling her?

But he wasn't saying a word now, just staring at her, the heat in his eyes incinerating her. She was sitting there, over chicken, feeling more on fire for anyone than she ever had in her life. She wanted to leap across the table, knock all the dishes off and jump in his lap. She wanted to forget about everything else that made her feel bad and scared. He made her feel good and safe.

He had a fantastic smile, and even when he wasn't smiling, he had a gorgeous mouth. And he was looking at her still in that liquid fire way he had about him.

"Okay," she said, hypnotized. "Tell me."

"I want to kiss you," he said.

She worked to gulp in air to keep her brain operating. Then she realized that those deep, simmering blue eyes of his were filled with a haunting vulnerability along with the heat.

"But I'm not going to kiss you," he went on. "Not unless you tell me you want me to. I'm not going to hit on you, Calla. I'm not like those other men you seem to judge us all by."

He wasn't like Brian. She knew that already. So why was it so hard for her to accept that he wasn't like any other men she'd known, either? He was different, she'd seen that from the start. And he wanted to kiss her, but wouldn't force it on her. He wasn't holding back because he didn't *want* her. He was holding back because he *respected* her.

And oh. My. God. That just made her want him more. She already felt like her system was on complete overload. Her head was going to blow up. Bam.

"I'm sorr—"

"Don't be sorry," he broke in. "Just give me a chance, Calla. If it's what you want, too."

Dane knew he wasn't playing completely fair. He'd lied to Calla, but not about how he felt about her. That was a basic truth. And seeing Brian grab for her with that knife in his hand had put him over the edge.

It could have all been over right then and there.

"Are you going to keep talking about it," she

said lightly, a little breathlessly, "or are you going to do something about it?"

He felt an odd tightness in his chest as he looked into her eyes. She was going to get emotionally involved if he kissed her. *He* was already emotionally involved and he hadn't even kissed her yet. He wanted love. He wanted to be loved. He wanted to be loved by Calla. He wanted home and hearth and family and a good, sweet woman who could be his partner. He wanted what he'd never had in his whole life. And he wanted it before it was too late.

"Yeah," he said. "I'm going to do something about it."

Her mouth trembled in a small smile, shy. God, he was shaking in his boots. When had a kiss ever been such a big deal?

She was so beautiful, with the electric light from the lantern-style fixture over the table accenting the shadows of her cheekbones and glimmering in her wide eyes as still she smiled up at him so shyly.

"Today?" she said finally.

He laughed—more an exhale than a laugh, but it took the edge off his nerves. Nerves. He was nervous, like a sixteen-year-old boy working up to his first kiss.

"Impatient?"

She bit her lip, that lip he wanted to be licking right now. "Sort of."

He was scared, that was the truth. What if it didn't turn out the way he thought it would? What if he was disappointed, or she was? It mattered, really mattered. *Calla* mattered.

Surely fate had put him here, in this position with Calla, because there weren't going to be fireworks when they kissed, *really* kissed. And he knew then there wasn't any doubt that kissing Calla would be better than wonderful. It was himself he doubted. She deserved better than him. But she was smiling at him still, and breaking his heart because he wanted her so bad.

She was wrong about him. He wasn't nice. He wasn't nice at all because he was going to take whatever she offered him tonight.

He pushed back his chair, but she was faster than him, and oh God, her lips were so sweet, her body so warm and soft. She twined her arms right around his neck, opened her mouth and invited him in. He kissed her back—slow, deep, giving her time to back off if she changed her mind, and praying to God she wouldn't at the same time.

Finally he lifted his mouth and stared down at her, captured by the dark eyes swimming with so much intensity meeting his, so much emotion it hurt to look. It terrified him, but he couldn't, didn't want to, look away.

"You're still thinking too much," he said raspily, his heart racing with the hot, dangerous heat she stirred so easily.

She slid one hand away from his neck, to his jawline, then his cheek, touching him in a wondering way. His arm angled over her hips, holding her snug, not wanting her to leave him.

"I just can't believe you," she said softly. "I'm afraid I made you up."

"I'm real," he said.

"I've dreamed about someone like you for a long time," she said. "Fantasized, I guess. A man who was patient and kind and respectful. Someone I didn't just want to sleep with, but someone I liked, too. I've never been able to find that. I tried for a while, but I gave up. Maybe too soon."

Her honesty humbled him. She wanted to sleep with him, and that humbled him, too.

"And now here you are." Her eyes were full now, liquid with that vulnerable emotion she was laying right on her sleeve for him to see.

"Here *you* are," he said back, and he kissed her again, because he couldn't help it, because he couldn't get enough of her, because he might cry if he didn't.

She made a sexy noise in her throat and with a moan he tore his mouth from her lips and placed it on her throat. His hands floated down, skimming her waist, her hips, needing to know every part of her, then she was kissing him again. And again.

"I want you naked," she stopped long enough to whisper.

So, so unbelievable. He was aroused, achingly so. He was yearning and burning for her, and not just his body, but his heart. He'd only known her for a few days, but he felt closer to her than he had to anyone in his life.

"You are so beautiful," he rasped, "and you smell so good, and I want you so bad—" He could hear the longing inside him making his voice rough and husky. This was too good, too intense, and if this whole thing was a big, long wet dream, he sure as hell hoped *now* wasn't going to be when he woke up.

She pressed another soul-wrenching kiss on him that blew what was left of his mind. He could kiss her all night if that was all she wanted, but she wanted more and that was really killing him.

"Calla." He tore his mouth from hers. She lifted

her wide-eyed gaze to his. His blood pumped fiercely and all he could think was that she was wearing way too many clothes. He swept his hands reverently down her body, begging himself for the control that was so sorely needed right now.

"I want you," she said, countering whatever argument he hadn't had the brain cell function to formulate yet. "I want you more than I have ever wanted a man in my whole entire life." Then she kissed him again, harder, hotter, even than before. She pulled back. "I want you naked. I want you on the table and I want you on the floor and I want you on the bed. I just want you."

Oh God. "Are you kidding?"

"No."

He kissed her face, her neck, her breasts right through the thick, soft material of her sweater. He wanted to get down on his knees and worship her. He wanted to take her clothes off with his teeth and lick every inch of her.

At her half sob, half laugh, he realized he had said that last bit out loud.

"I want you to do that, too," she whispered raggedly. "And I want you to hurry."

He was really, really sorry they'd taken that mattress out of here.

"There's chicken," he said, as if he could stand it if she wanted to stop and finish dinner.

"I like chicken cold," she said.

"I really like you," he said.

"I know." And the smile that spread across her face made him want to stare at her forever, but she took his hand and pulled him after her. She led him to the bedroom, the room where he'd spent that first night here, and she turned. A long, achy beat passed and she said, "Well, time's a-wastin'."

And he laughed so hard, he thought he might choke and then she reached for him, tugged him down onto the bed after her so he landed on top of her, barely managing to brace himself in time so he didn't crush her.

He didn't want to hurt her in any way—not ever. He saw in her eyes, so close as she lay beneath him, the depth and intensity that he'd come to expect from her, and other things. Things he could guess. Her fears, her hopes. Moving slightly to the side so he could see her more, he gently, tentatively, ran his hand over her sweater, felt the hard tips of her nipples—no bra—poking beneath the material.

"Calla—"

The permission he sought, she gave. She reached up, took his hand, slid it deliberately beneath her sweater, against the bare skin of her belly, and higher. She made a low, sexy moan as he moved his hand up, covered one breast, cupping the soft, full sweetness of her. She wriggled, reached between them, tore the sweater over her head, leaving her chest and belly naked and he was just about mindless.

Her eyes shone up at him in the darkness of the bedroom. No lamps were on in here. They hadn't stopped for that. The moon had risen and deep blue light, soft and almost magical, floated around them through the gauzy lace of the curtained window. She was more lovely than he could believe.

She reached for the zipper of his jeans, tore at the buttons of his borrowed flannel shirt. He helped her, rolling over to tear his clothes off then sitting back, awed, as she rose to pull down her pants. She stood there in front of him, bathed in that ethereal moon glow, in nothing but little tiny panties, breathtakingly beautiful from her soft shoulders to her narrow waist and the gentle bloom of her hips ending in long, long legs he wanted curled right around his waist, right now and forever more.

Then she took the panties off, too.

Coming back to the bed, she pushed him down

and climbed on top of him, straddling him and said, "I'm scared."

Oh, man. He would stop now. He would do whatever she wanted even if it killed him, even if she was sitting on him naked while she said it.

"It's okay," he said, dying.

"I don't mean I want to stop," she said. "I mean, I'm scared that I—"

She stopped, blinked fast and he realized those were tears in her eyes.

"Calla—"

"I'm scared I won't please you," she said all in a rush.

"You already please me," he said, stunned. "You can't do anything that *won't* please me. I promise you that." He slid his hands to her waist, folding her close to him and she slipped down, laid her head on his chest. He could feel the tautness of her nipples against his bare skin, hear the pounding of her heart, smell the sweet, delicious scent of her hair. And he didn't know why she was still so scared, but he knew he could hold her until she was ready, would hold her as long as she wanted.

Finally she lifted her face.

"There's just something I have to tell you first," she whispered.

Chapter 15

"You can tell me anything," he said.

Could she? He touched her face, pulled her down gently to kiss him, so tenderly. Calla's heart did a circus act in her chest. Here she was in bed with a man she'd only met a few days ago, and yet it felt so right.

And yet she was so scared, of being wrong, of finding out something was wrong with *her*.

"I haven't had sex in a really long time," she said. "Not for several years, to be honest." She pushed off him, sat beside him on the bed.

He raised up, sat beside her, laying his hand on

her arm, very gently, nonthreatening. It was up to her what she told him, what happened next. He left everything up to her, and it made her feel safe even as she risked more than she ever had before.

"Brian said hurtful things to me in bed," she said, staring down at her hands, drawing up her knees. Hiding her nakedness even in the dark. "He told me that something was wrong with me."

"Your ex-husband was an ass, not to mention criminally insane. I think tonight proved that."

"He told me I didn't like sex."

"He didn't deserve that gift from you," J.D. said quietly. "And he has no idea if you like sex or not. Only you know that, Calla."

She swallowed thickly. "But I don't know." It should have been strange—sitting in bed naked with a man, a naked man, discussing her painful insecurities. But it didn't feel strange at all with J.D. It felt perfect. It was difficult because the emotions were still raw despite all the years since she'd divorced Brian, but it felt cathartic, too. And she trusted J.D. not to judge her.

"After it was over between me and Brian, I had a few relationships. Affairs, really. I thought they would make me feel better, but they only made me feel worse. They were just…physical. I didn't like myself for doing it, so I stopped. And I've been afraid ever since that the fact that I could stop, just stop and never have sex at all, meant that maybe Brian was right. Maybe I don't like sex."

"Or maybe you just haven't had sex with the right man," J.D. offered. "Someone you were on the same page with as far as how you felt emotionally. Someone you liked. Someone you were having sex with for more than physical reasons."

What was he saying now? Her heart felt tight, achy.

"I like you, Calla," he went on softly. "I like who you are and how you are. I want to get to know you better, and I'm interested in you for more than sex. There's nothing you can possibly do that will disappoint me, even if what you do is choose to wait and not make love with me tonight. Making love with you is a privilege, not something I expect."

They were sitting here naked and he would stop. He wouldn't tell her there was something wrong with her if she wasn't ready. He wouldn't insist on his way. He thought making love with her was a gift, a privilege.

"If this is some kind of reverse psychology," she said, "it's working." She was so hot for him, she might spontaneously combust.

His glittering gaze, intense and kind, held hers.

"I don't know what you're doing to me," she said, "but you're making me burn up inside, I want you so bad."

"I'm not doing anything," he said.

"I know." She laughed. "That is what is so weird about it." She sobered then. "I want you to kiss me. I want you to touch me. I want you inside of me."

Heat bloomed, deeper inside her, just saying the words.

She lay back, staring up at him beside her in the shadows. He looked at her for a long beat, as if he might study her forever, then his hand moved to her thigh, and thinking became difficult as his fingers traced their way upward, sliding over the mound of short curls there, to her belly, her breasts. Her nipples waited for him, tight and greedy already. He moved to lay beside her, kiss her on the mouth as his fingers continued to tease and torment her aching peaks.

"Do you like that, Calla?" he whispered against her mouth.

"Yes." Oh God. *Yes*.

His fingers slipped lower and he kissed and licked his way down to her belly button. Splaying his hand over her most private part, she felt heat pooling between her legs and she moved them apart, granting him access. He moved his fingers into the slick need of her and she moaned, reached for his shoulders, then the sheet beside her, desperate as his talented, knowing torture sent the world madly spinning.

"Do you like that, Calla?"

"Oh, yes," she breathed.

Then he moved lower, sucked her into his mouth with his tongue, his teeth, rocking her with pleasure until she cried out, shameless, dizzily letting go. She spiraled into some deep, sweet world of insistent need and exploding heat. She could think of nothing but what he was doing to her and how much she did, oh she did, like it, and then she couldn't even think of that.

She lay there like a limp noodle, shaking and understanding finally what the "little death" meant. Oh yeah, she'd died. Died and gone to heaven.

"Did you like that, Calla?" His voice came out rough, raspy, like he was as turned on as she even though she had, she realized guiltily, done nothing for him. Yet.

She remembered when she tried to answer him that you had to be able to breathe in order to speak. What she wanted to tell him was that she was going to die if she didn't have more, more and more of him, that was how much she liked it.

Condom. The word seared her brain.

She burst up, suddenly inspired to strength despite the wobbly, hot, liquid state of her bones. In less than a heartbeat, she'd found her jeans in the dark, found the pocket, found Meg's presents, and was back.

"I like it so much," she said shakily, eagerly, "I want to do it all night. Can we do it all night?"

J.D. laughed. "We can do it as much as you want, Calla. We can do it tonight. We can do it tomorrow. We can do it the day after that, too. Let's make that an appointment, Miss Jones. I'll put you in my book."

Oh boy.

Slowly, wordlessly, she pulled him down on top of her, kissing him with every bit of passion that was burning up every cell in her body. He returned her kisses with the same fiery need. His body felt powerful and muscular to her exploring hands. She felt dizzyingly limp and startlingly alive all at once. He answered her back, exploration for exploration, as fierce and impatient as she.

"Don't stop," she begged when he pulled away. "Please don't stop." She was panting and dying for him. Dying for him to be inside her. Aching all over.

"I'm coming back," he promised, and she

realized he'd taken up the little package she'd brought to the bed.

He came back to her, just as he'd said he would, and she ran her hands over his back, pulling him down over her, wrapping her legs around him. She never wanted to let go. She arched her hips to him, watched his eyes fire as she reached between them, grasped his manhood. Even then, he didn't sink into her, intent on driving her completely mad as he now reached between them, too, stroking her to the edge of insanity. Seconds, or maybe hours, passed as they touched and kissed and stroked and loved before finally, finally, in one slow, hot glide, he entered her.

Intense pleasure drowned her, just like that, building so quickly she could scarcely believe it. She whimpered, clinging to him, arching against him and begging for more, holding on for dear life, holding him in deep, just holding him there. There. Where she would happily keep him forever.

He began to move and ripples of bliss rolled over her, taking her right out of herself. She exploded with a cry and he was right behind her. He held her tight, held her as she floated back down, held her as it hit her what had happened, hit her that she knew, really finally knew, that she was okay, that there was nothing wrong with her. Held her while she sobbed. Just held her and stroked her and kissed her and didn't say a word.

They must have slept that way, still a part of each other, because she remembered waking to find him disengaging their bodies, moving to the side, cradling her against him where she fell asleep again. When she woke the second time, he was gone and she was alone. She lay there, stretching, smiling, knowing she'd never been so relaxed in her life. She felt good about him, about herself. She liked herself, and she liked him. She liked everything about him, from his sexy kindness to his powerful body to his oh-so-hot voice. Just thinking about his voice made her melt all over and want him again. Tonight. Tomorrow. The day after that.

Her eyes flashed open and she froze.

She *had* heard his voice before, and suddenly she remembered when.

Dane opened the laptop in Calla's second bedroom. Setapraxin. The name of the drug Calla said she'd worked on had kept bugging him, niggling at the back of his mind. She'd said the drug she'd worked on had failed. He only worked with drugs that had reached the point where they were being prepared for market.

He powered on the computer, breathed a sigh

of relief when he discovered there was no password into the system and forcibly pushed aside the
guilt of using her laptop without permission. He
was doing this *for* Calla and he would explain
everything soon, he hoped. The operating system
loaded, and he clicked on the Internet icon. Calla
had been sleeping when he left her, but he didn't
know how much time he had—and that was a
concern in more than one sense. Today was
December 22.

If what had happened with Brian was different
from before and had happened only because he
was here and had caused Brian to snap, then it was
still possible that there were other things this time
that were the same. Like, that today was the day
Calla would be murdered. He couldn't just put
the danger down to Brian and forget about it. His
chest went tight. Saving Calla meant more to him
than ever. After last night, the thought of losing
her—he couldn't stand it.

Moving as quickly as the dial-up service allowed, he typed in the page that brought up the
company Web site. Clicking on the log-in screen,
he put in his username and password to access the
company's private network. From here, he could
access his own files, and he pulled up the list of
drugs in his current database, some still in the

process of receiving FDA approval and others that had already passed. There was no setapraxin.

He left the company site and did a quick Internet search. No setapraxin. Back to the company Web site and his own files in the network. So why did he know that name? He clicked open one drug's history file and ran a quick "find" task on setapraxin. Nothing. He clicked through two more then sat back, stared at the screen. He felt a tingle at his nape and he knew something was wrong, very wrong.

And God, he had a sinking feeling what it could be but he couldn't believe it at the same time.

Lexitocin. He'd been working on it for a year. The files on it were perfect. It was an outstanding drug with enormous potential. It would make millions for Ledger Pharmaceuticals and virtually wipe out breast cancer.

Lexitocin had had a previous name during the research phase.

Lexitocin was setapraxin.

And setapraxin cured cancer but over time destroyed heart function.

Ledger was trying to put a drug on the market that would kill the very women it was saving. The wonder drug that killed.

The confidentiality agreement…

It was useless. Calla would never keep silent about a drug that could kill, confidentiality agreement or not. So why had Carter Sloane been so insistent about sending Dane to Haven to get it?

The air whooshed out of his chest and it wasn't long before he realized something pretty terrifying.

Someone had needed to take the fall for Calla's death. Had it all been that simple? Carter Sloane had changed the name of the drug, dismissed every assistant who'd worked on the project, but he needed Calla out of the way. Calla had been the project head. Calla had taken her findings to the company chief without sharing them with anyone else. The project had been canceled with no explanation. Further trials had been done, but none of the studies were of a duration that would show the flaw Calla had found in her basic research.

Calla was the only one who knew.

And he'd been... Handy? An easy fall guy? Disposable? Send the lawyer out to see the former researcher. No one would care if he got nailed for a crime he *hadn't* committed. He had no life, no close friends, no family to give a rat's ass. Make it look like a crime of passion. No one would be able to testify that he hadn't had an affair with Calla. No one knew him well enough.

Bitter anger followed up hot terror. Was it that simple, that ugly? And Carter Sloane, the same Carter Sloane who had been so generous about standing by his employee, who had hired his defense team, who had come to his trial... Carter Sloane had set him up?

He thought back to that day again, the day he'd come to Haven Christmas Tree Farm. He remembered pulling into the driveway, taking in the fields, the barn, the house. He'd walked up to the house, knocked on the door. Calla had answered. He'd gone inside, then... He'd asked her if he could use her phone. His cell didn't work out here in the boonies and Calla had claimed she didn't need to sign the paper, claimed there was one in her file already. It had been a general document, not specific to any one project. He'd never mentioned lexitocin in their conversation.

He'd gone to the phone while she'd said customers were arriving and she had business to take care of. He'd come out of the house, been struck on the head, and when he'd woken up, found a gun in his hand and Calla's body riddled with bullets, blood everywhere, stark on the white snow.

Fool that he'd been, he'd called 911 and never anticipated what would happen next, that *he* would be charged with the crime.

A shiver suddenly whisked through his body. This was December 22. And Calla was about to die.

Call 911. Call the police. Call them *now*.

He reached for the phone. He'd call the police, then he'd explain to Calla, tell her anything, anything he could tell her that would get her out of this house, into her truck, into Haven.

He had to get her away from this farm. He had to tell her about the lexatocin/setapraxin connection.

The rest of his story…God, he had no idea how to tell her that. A sound behind him told him he'd taken too long, and listened too little.

"You got your memory back," Calla said, and he turned, saw that she was staring at him, saw in the baffled look on her face that she had seen the company network open on the screen. Saw, too, that whatever trust she had placed in him was severely shaken now. "Or did you ever lose it?"

"Calla—"

"What do you want, Mr. McGuire? Or should I call you Dane? We did sleep together."

His heart tore as her voice broke on that last bit.

Chapter 16

Calla stood there, facing him, hurt, so much hurt, swimming inside her eyes. She looked sick, scared—of him. His heart sank even as his blood pressure rocked off the charts.

"I kept thinking," she said, and her voice wobbled even as he could see her take a deep breath, work to harden her words. "I kept thinking I knew your voice. You made an appointment with me. You called me on the phone. You're from Ledger. And here you are, on the company network online. You know who you are."

"Yes."

"How long have you known?"

Trust was so fragile. Trust was everything with Calla. She'd placed it, for the first time in years, with him. And he could see, even now, a desperate hope on her face. But he couldn't lie to her now, not even if it would keep her from hating him. He knew who wanted her dead. And she had to know, too. It was her life that mattered now, not what she thought of him.

"From the beginning."

She squeezed her eyes shut and he could almost see the air whoosh out of her as the pain sunk in.

"Why?"

"I was scared." He rose, stepped toward her, stopped as she opened her eyes, backed up. "I wasn't thinking straight. I didn't know what had happened to me, what *was* happening to me. I didn't know who I could trust."

He'd been scared of Calla at first, wondered if she was part of some mad plot to make him think he was crazy. He couldn't have been more wrong.

"I was wrong," he told her. His heart filled his throat. He didn't have time to argue with her. She didn't have time. "I should have told you the truth, but I didn't think you'd believe me." He grabbed her by the shoulders before she could back away again. "You have to believe me now, Calla. Your life is in danger."

"What are you talking about? They took Brian in. He's probably the one who shot at me from the woods. There isn't any other danger! There isn't anyone who wants to hurt me—no one else."

"It's not Brian! And you didn't know about Brian wanting to hurt you. There are other things you don't know about, too, Calla. There is someone who has a reason to want you dead. And I know who it is now. We don't have time. We have to call the police and get the hell out of here." And not necessarily in that order.

She wouldn't budge when he tried to take her hand.

"You said something, something after I first brought you to the house. Something about the ones who did this to you, the ones who killed me."

He could feel her body trembling under his hands.

"We have to get out of here, Calla."

"I'm not going anywhere. Not until you tell me the truth. The whole truth this time!"

"You won't believe it."

"Try me. Because I'm not going anywhere until you do."

He'd lost her trust. Just like that, all the trust

was gone. And he was scared to death he couldn't gain it back in time.

He didn't want to tell her things that would only frighten her more. Things she would never believe.

"Ledger is going ahead with setapraxin. Only they're calling it lexitocin now."

She gasped. "That's insane. It'll kill people."

"I know that now. But that's not what the trials show. That's only in your research, your basic research. Did you tell anyone else on your team what you discovered?"

"No. I went straight to Carter Sloane. I took full responsibility. He fired me, dismissed the whole team. I was escorted from the building." Her voice broke slightly. "I never spoke to any of them again. They couldn't be trying to put that drug on the market!"

"The trials show miraculous results," he said. "It's going to make it to market."

"It's going to kill people! I won't let that happen."

"Exactly."

Her eyes bulged. "Are you saying Carter Sloane wants me dead?"

"That's exactly what I'm saying. And he's coming here today to make it happen."

She backed up now, her spine hitting the doorjamb, her face bloodless. "How do you know?" He could almost see her mind racing. "Why did you come here? What happened to you?"

"I was sent here on a fool's mission, to get you to sign this confidentiality agreement. I'm going to be set up for the murder. I'm going to be hit on the head. He's going to shoot you, Calla. He's going to murder you in cold blood and just as coldly he's going to frame me for it, put the gun in my hand, make it look like a crime of passion. He's going to shoot you five times, Calla, and I'm going to go to prison. But not if we get out of here, right now, and go to the authorities."

She was shaking like a leaf. "How do you know all this?" she whispered tautly. "Oh, my God." She put her hand to her throat. "You're a part of it. You were in on it."

"No, I wasn't in on it, Calla! Trust me. Please, Calla, believe me."

"How else would you know all of this?"

Oh God. She might believe him about Ledger's plans for setapraxin and even about Carter Sloane, but the rest—

There was only one way he could explain how he knew so much, make her know that he wasn't in on it.

"Do you remember the earthquake last year?"

She blinked. "What?"

"That nonsense about the earthquake releasing positive ions that could trigger paranormal activity, you remember that?"

"Yes."

His blood ran ice-cold as he spoke. "It's true. Anything can happen in Haven. Something happened to me."

"What are you talking about?" Her voice came out shaky, small.

He was afraid to move toward her again, afraid she might scream, or run. He was scaring her, he could see that. He didn't have time to offer comfort, even as he felt the hot, sweet pull of her, the rawness of her emotion and his. He'd built trust with her, slowly, achingly, and now he was destroying it. But nothing mattered now besides her life.

Her throat moved and she looked poised for flight. He forced calm into his voice, calm he didn't feel. He had to make her see that he was telling her the truth.

"Do you remember that receipt you found on me?" She said nothing, just nodded, her eyes, so beautiful, so wary and huge. "It wasn't a mistake. It wasn't some duplicate number that erroneously appeared in the book. It was real. I had a suit dry-cleaned on June 7 of next year at that store. It was the suit I was wearing when you found me. I wore it to court, for my trial. My trial for your murder."

She gave a sharp gasp. "That's crazy! That would mean—"

"I came back in time, Calla." Now he did move, grab hold of her shoulders. She felt fragile and frightened under his hands. "I came back. I don't know how it happened, or why. One second I was riding in the back of a prison transport van on that June night after my sentencing, and the next I was thrown onto the snowy ground by the road outside your farm. Thrown back in time, six months. The transport van was in an accident. It was a stormy night. I felt this strange, humming pressure. The positive ions? I don't know, Calla! I just know that I came back in time. I know that you are going to be killed. I know that I am going to be set up for your murder. And now I know who is going to do it!"

He could see her throat work, the horror in her eyes slashing into his heart. His voice didn't come out calm now. It came out desperate, raspy.

"You have to believe me, Calla. You have to come with me, now. Today is the day. You were killed on December 22. I came to your house. I was struck on the head. I blacked out. When I woke, a gun was in my hand and you were dead.

It's not too late to stop it. We'll go to the police. We'll—"

"I'm not going anywhere with you! You're insane!" Her wild pulsebeat was visible. She was scared, scared of him, too scared to process what he was telling her. "You're crazy, and you're a liar. You made love to me while you were lying to me!"

"Nothing I said to you last night was a lie! Trust me, Calla."

"Everything you said to me last night was a lie," she countered. "I don't know what you want. I don't know why you came up with this crazy story. I don't know why you're really here. I just want you gone!"

Guilt stabbed him. He *had* lied to her. He *had* broken her trust. And God, he'd been too selfish, too desperate for the love he'd never known, to tell her the truth before. Too focused on not failing to protect her body to realize he was failing to protect her heart. It was *he* who hadn't trusted *her*, too afraid of losing her love.

Love. God. He *loved* her.

That blew his mind. "Calla—"

"Get away from me! I don't want to have anything to do with you, ever again!"

She shook off his hold, hit his chest with her hand, rocking him off balance as she took him by surprise.

"Calla!" He stumbled back, got his balance, reached for her—

Too late.

Calla was off like a shot. Keys. She grabbed at them where they hung on the peg in the hall. Her purse— Didn't know where it was, didn't care. She'd go to the police, all right. But not with J.D. Or Dane. Or whoever the hell he was.

Dammit. Her heart ripped inside her, but she kept running. Running from him and his lies and his insanity. He'd been too good to be true.

She should have known.

Ledger— She had no idea what to think of what he'd said about setapraxin. She'd find out. But now, all she wanted was to get away from him and the mangled heap he'd made of her heart.

She might as well have had the power to walk through walls, she made it to the door so fast, stumbling around the wreckage of the front room and onto the porch. Everything hit her at once. Snow, blindingly white. A car in front of the barn. Customers. It was too early for customers. For once she didn't care about business, either. Haven Christmas Tree Farm was closed today. People would just have to deal.

He was behind her and she wasn't stopping.

She never saw him before he grabbed her arm. Her heart tripped, jumped into her throat.

"Good morning, Miss Jones."

Carter Sloane. He must have been to the side of the door. He'd come out of nowhere, stopped her before she could leave the porch. Barking sounded, and suddenly there was Chuck, bounding around her ankles, sniffing at the Ledger chief.

"Mr. Sloane." She couldn't think. Dane. Where was Dane? He'd been right behind her. Now all she knew was the rushing of blood in her ears. "What are you doing here?" Her voice came out thin, strangled.

Oh God. She was going to be killed today. *Was that true?* Killed by Carter Sloane?

"My company attorney has an appointment with you this morning, is that right?"

"Yes."

She'd always thought he was kind of grandfatherly, in an austere way. Carter Sloane was a meticulous dresser, always perfectly groomed. But kind and sometimes even generous. The day he'd fired her, she'd been shocked, but how easy it had been to simply blame herself despite knowing that it had been a mistake, one anyone could have missed, and that it was extreme for her to lose her job over it.

If what Dane had said was true, that Sloane fired her so he could release the drug, flaw and all, that made a sick sense. But she still couldn't wrap her mind around the idea that he would knowingly release a drug that could kill.

Couldn't wrap her mind around the idea that he would be willing to kill *her*.

"I see he's not here yet. I'll wait, if you don't mind."

Escape. That was all she could think. She had to get out of here. *Where was Dane?*

Sloane didn't realize Dane was here. He would have expected him to come in his own vehicle, she realized with a start.

"I have to go. I'm sorry."

"But we have an appointment."

"It's canceled." Canceled permanently.

The Ledger chief was still holding on to her arm. "It can't be canceled. It's too important."

"Well, I'm sorry, but it is canceled." She tried to free her arm.

No chance. He wouldn't release her.

She bit back a protest. Scared, so scared suddenly and sharply. He would not let go of her, she knew that, viscerally.

He was not going to let her leave this farm. Chuck stretched out on the porch step. Old dog.

No help. She wanted to scream for him to attack this crazy man, the real crazy man, holding on to her arm. Knew it would do no good.

"We should go inside," he said.

Inside, where he could kill her in cold blood. Think. She had to think!

He was here expecting Dane to arrive. Expecting to set Dane up for her murder.

Shock rolled over her in reeling waves. Was everything Dane said the truth? The receipt— The receipt dated six months from now. Setapraxin and lexitocin. Carter Sloane.

The Ledger chief was here, she knew that. And she knew he wasn't going to let her leave. Where was Dane?

If he was smart, he was laying low. She hadn't believed him. She'd run away from him. She'd told him she didn't want anything to do with him, ever again.

But that was unfair. He wasn't laying low to save his own life, or running away. Not Dane. If he'd wanted to run away, to save himself, he could have run away before. He didn't have to come back to her farm yesterday. He hadn't had to do anything he'd done.

He'd risked his own life to save her. All the hurt, all the doubt, turned to instant regret. He was for real. He was different. He'd wanted to help her, to save her—if all he wanted to do was save himself, he'd have made damn sure he was nowhere near her on this day, the day she would be killed.

Dread backed up in her throat. Her heart hammered wildly.

Dane was inside the house. He had to have darted back when Carter Sloane had appeared in the open doorway. He had to have seen him. He had to be waiting, inside.

He had to be believing in her, believing she was smart enough and strong enough to do the right thing, to help him help her. Dane believed in her, believed she was strong and smart and capable. Dane, who she liked so much, who liked her back, who was different, after all. He would believe in her.

And she had to believe in him. He'd said Carter had shot her outside, but that wasn't going to happen now. Not now that Carter believed he had arrived before Dane. He would shoot her inside, after Dane arrived, or even before Dane arrived—while waiting for him to get there, waiting to frame him. He expected Dane to arrive any minute. Her mind worked, stumbling over possible scenarios.

"It's cold out here, Miss Jones." The Ledger chief pushed her slightly, toward the doorway. "We'll wait inside."

She swallowed thickly. "Okay."

Where could Dane be waiting? Where? She turned toward the door. The inside of the farmhouse lay in shadows. The front room was wrecked. That would give her an excuse to walk Sloane through the house. Give Dane an opportunity to take him down.

Or Sloane an opportunity to shoot her dead.

Trust me. Oh God. She would. She would trust Dane with her life. If he deserved to know nothing else, if everything went terribly wrong, he deserved to know that truth. She trusted him. And all she could do was pray she had a chance to tell him she more than trusted him. She believed him and she loved him.

The house lay still and frightening before her. The front door made a bang behind them. Sloane must have pulled it shut.

"A tree came through the roof," she said to Sloane. "We can wait in the kitchen." They would walk by the hall, the hall to the bedrooms. Please, God, let Dane be there.

She fought for control, fought to keep herself from looking to either side as she walked. Sloane had let go of her arm, but he was right behind her, so close she knew she'd never get a step away from him if she tried to run.

When she passed the opening to the hall going back to the bedrooms, she stopped, pivoted sharply. The Ledger chief nearly bumped into her, he was that close.

"I just want to know something," she said. Her voice shook. She struggled, took a deep breath. Forced herself not to react, in any way. Behind him, just inside the hall, stood a solid shape, Dane, in the shadows.

He held something in his hands. Something heavy. She couldn't see what it was. Hope unfurled in her chest even as she knew everything could go terribly wrong even now.

Distract Sloane. Keep him distracted. "Why are you releasing setapraxin as lexitocin?" she said all in a rush. "What makes you think you can get away with—"

"So you know that, do you, Miss Jones? It'll be years before the drug's flaw becomes evident. Years before the lawsuits roll in. By then, I'll be living in Brazil off the millions that will be rolling in to Ledger, my well-deserved bonus as CEO for putting the wonder drug on the market."

Her head spun even as she saw Dane moving closer. She wanted to shout out to him that she loved him, so terrified she'd never get the chance. She knew he wasn't the one who was insane. She'd been so wrong and she could only pray it wasn't too late. Carter Sloane was the one who was insane. "You're crazy," she said to him.

"Like a fox." Suddenly there was a gun, glinting through the shadows of the front room, in Carter Sloane's hand.

Dizziness hit her. She couldn't breathe. Then it all happened so fast and she realized she had been wrong again. And so had Dane.

When Carter spoke, he wasn't speaking to her.

"You should have let me shoot her in the woods. Then you wouldn't have had to die, too. Now I'll have to make it look like a robbery, and that you were both killed," he said as he pivoted because he knew, God, he knew, that Dane was already here.

All she knew was heartbreak as the gun blasted.

Chapter 17

The shot deafened Dane, knocking him back in the dark hall. Then he heard Calla screaming, Chuck barking and scratching at the front door. His shoulder burned, on fire, even as euphoria hit him. He'd saved Calla. He would still save Calla. She was alive and whole, and he was going to keep her that way. He'd rather die than go to prison, and he'd rather die than let anything happen to Calla. Give Calla time to run.

Keep Sloane's attention on him. That was the ticket.

He struggled back to his feet, almost superhuman

adrenaline driving him over the pain, even as Carter Sloane advanced on him, the gun trained on his chest.

"Run!" he gasped at Calla even as he saw her hesitate, and his heart exploded as she finally did run. She was going to make it, thank God.

Carter shot again, and he lunged to the side, the bullet screaming past his ear. He lost his balance, dizziness soaking him suddenly. Blood. He was losing blood, fast. All he could feel was wet heat washing down his arm from his shoulder.

"She's not going anywhere," Carter said madly. "I made sure of that already. Her truck won't run. I slashed her tires before I came in here."

Oh God. He'd shoot him dead any second and Calla would have barely made it to her truck in the garage. He'd shoot her before she could get back out and run for the woods or the road.

He'd lost and Carter had won. Again. Agony, not just physical, sickened him.

The Ledger chief was a blur in the shadows. A blur raising that gun again, this time at his head. He reduced to a tiny prick of light, savage light, in his eyes as he prepared to fire. Dane felt himself slipping down the wall. He wasn't superhuman, after all.

Then there was another blur. A blur behind Sloane, hurling something heavy and long. She slammed it into the back of Sloane's head. The older man rocked forward, stumbled, but still managed to fire off that last shot.

Dane hit the floor, new pain ripping into him.

"Don't die, don't die," Calla begged as she raced to his side. In the pinprick of sight he retained as the world slipped away, he saw her face, her beautiful face, heard her voice pleading with him.

Then she was gone and so was the world.

Calla paced outside the double doors that led into the emergency room of the hospital in Haven. She would never forget the mind-numbing terror of seeing Dane collapse, seeing all that blood soaking through his clothes. Seeing him slip away right before her very eyes.

Couldn't forget it because she felt it still, right now, waiting desperately for the surgeon's report. Waiting to find out if Dane had survived.

Sloane was alive after she'd hit him on the head with a piece of debris from the roof collapse and that was far more than he deserved. She'd called the police, and thank God they'd arrived before the Ledger chief had woken up, but if they hadn't, she had known without a shadow of a doubt that she could have done what she'd never done before.

She could have used that gun she'd picked up after she'd knocked him unconscious. She could have and would have shot him if she'd had to.

It was over now, over except for the crime scene that was now her home. The police promised she'd be able to go into the house later today, after they'd finished retrieving forensics evidence, taking pictures. Sloane would go on trial. That part wouldn't be over for a long time. But the drug that could kill wouldn't go on the market now. Innocent people wouldn't die.

Unless Dane— Her heart ached so badly.

The waiting room was merrily decked out in Christmas wreaths and bows. Merry Christmas was spelled out in red cutout letters on the wall. It was nearly empty this midmorning only a few days before Christmas. She thought of the Charlie Brown tree they'd taken back together to the farmhouse, decorated. How then they'd made love. The sweetest, kindest love she'd ever known.

Dane. He had a name; finally he had a name. He'd been so patient with her, and she'd held back, not believing in him, not believing he was real. She hoped it wasn't too late. Hoped he would give her another chance— Hoped *he* had another chance.

The surgeon came through the double doors. She stood, her knees shaking.

"Is he—" The words caught in her throat. Blood roared in her ears.

"Mr. McGuire made it through surgery. We were able to remove the bullets. He's in the ICU now—"

Hot relief hit her, nearly buckling her knees. "Can I see him?" She had to fight the urge to blast right past the surgeon, blaze into the ICU.

"He's asking for you."

And then she raced right past him. She'd waited long enough, too long. The surgeon was right behind her. He reached for her arm as she made it through the double doors.

"This way, Miss Jones," he said gently. "This way."

And he was there, in a hospital bed, low-lit, tubes and wires everywhere, but she saw none of that. Saw only Dane. Alive! Emotions came at her and a sob filled her throat as her feet flew to the bedside.

She stopped short, suddenly scared—of how he felt, of how she felt.

He looked so pale. She sat on the chair by the bed. His eyes were closed. The machine beside the bed beeped and hummed quietly.

She looked up at the surgeon standing at the foot of the bed. "Is it okay—if I talk to him?" she whispered.

He smiled gently. "Yes, it's okay. He's conscious, in and out. Don't stay too long."

She swallowed thickly. "I promise."

He nodded, turned away. The humming and beeping of the machine filled her ears. She reached up, laid her hand softly over Dane's.

Bandages crossed both shoulders, the sheet pulled to halfway up his chest. Despite the obvious signs of surgery, he looked every bit the lean, powerful man he had when she'd first found him, even hypothermic. His eyes were closed in his wonderfully kind, handsome face, the lines of his features chiseled and beloved now, no longer a stranger. No longer a stranger even before she'd known his name, she realized as she softly stroked his hand.

"Hi," the raw whisper came, and her gaze flashed to his face again. His overpoweringly hot and sexy eyes were just as warm as ever, despite the exhaustion and effort she could see him making to speak. "I missed you."

She felt something hot hit her cheek. Knew she was crying. Didn't care. She pressed the fingers of her other hand to her mouth, stifled a sob.

"Hi." Her voice broke on the word. "I missed you, too. I was so scared." Everything, all the emotions, the fear and the hope, choked her throat.

"Don't be scared," he said. "Don't be scared ever again, Calla."

"Not anymore. Not with you." She cried softly. And she wasn't then, couldn't be, not with his wonderful, kind eyes on hers. Trust, so fragile and yet so strong. "I love you," she breathed.

He smiled. Weakly, beautifully, happily. "Don't stop doing that," he said.

"I won't. I can't. I'm so sorry," she burst out suddenly. "I should have believed you. I should have known—"

"You couldn't," he insisted, his gaze turning tormented now. "I should have told you before. I should have known I could trust you. I was scared, too, Calla. I never knew anyone like you. My parents, my whole life, have always been off on some expedition or another, studying—whatever. I'm a loner. I'm a loner who doesn't want to be alone anymore, and that scared me so badly, I didn't know what to do with it but try to pretend it wasn't happening. Try to pretend I wasn't falling in love with you."

Her heart nearly burst from her chest. "I love you, too."

"I know." He smiled again, this time hugely, and she could see tears glimmering in his dark, deep eyes, too. Joyful tears.

"I want to live with you on your mountain," he said. "Forever. Will you let me?"

Forever. Oh God, she loved that word. She couldn't speak, could only raise up, meet him as he lifted his arm, wires dangling down from his wrist, to crush his mouth where he lay. Then she was shaking and crying and he was kissing every tear. She finally pulled back, scared she'd hurt him.

"Don't go away," he whispered.

"I'm not. Never!"

"I don't understand what happened," he said, intense, suddenly. "I don't know how or why I came back in time. But I believe, I really believe, I didn't just come back to save myself from prison or even just to save your life. I came back for this." His searing gaze locked with hers. "I came back because we were meant to be together, Calla. It's too right, too real. Positive ions, or magic, whatever it was. I came back for you."

Tears fell faster down her cheeks. She didn't understand what had happened, either. But she believed it, believed in him. Her heart knew it had to be true.

"You could have just left town," she said thickly, stroking his dear face, his cheek, his jaw. "You could have just saved yourself. Then this wouldn't have happened." He wouldn't have been shot, nearly killed. The enormity of the risk he'd taken for her rose in her mind, left her head nearly reeling. "You could have ended up in prison again."

"I couldn't have left you," he said simply. "Wouldn't."

She was inches from his shining eyes. She could feel his body, hard and hot, beneath her. He was going to be all right. He was going to recover.

He was going to come home to Haven Christmas Tree Farm—with her. Her very own Christmas gift. A bubble of happiness rose in her chest.

"But—" She stared at him sharply, worried now. "You work for Ledger. You're an attorney."

"I don't care. I'll open a private practice in Haven. I'll cut Christmas trees down in the winter and drive the Appaloosas to take customers sledding and plant pumpkins with you for the fall. I want to do it all—with you. If you'll let me."

Let him? She laughed, so happy she could barely stand it. But oh, she would learn to stand it. She would learn to stand being happy. Not a problem.

He was everything she'd hoped for even when she wouldn't let herself know she was hoping. He wasn't a soap opera scenario. He was a dream. A dream come true.

"You know what the best part is?" she asked softly. "I like you. I really like you. And then I love you, too."

"I like you, too, Calla. That's what makes the loving so much better."

She laughed again, pressed another sweet, sweet kiss on his mouth. "Yeah," she breathed. "Everything about you is so much better than I ever imagined." A slice of guilt hit her as she realized she was putting her weight on him and she backed off an inch. All she could stand to, just enough to get her weight off him. "You must be in pain," she said.

"Drugs," he said. "Good drugs."

Between them, in his eyes, she could see what she knew, too. How close Ledger had come to putting a killer drug on the market. A drug that wasn't good at all.

"Hey, we saved the world," he said quietly. "We must be doing something right."

She smiled, kissed him again. "Yeah. I think we're doing something right. More than right. The best."

"The best," he promised, "is yet to come."

Epilogue

The best started three days later, at 7:02 p.m. when Dane walked into Calla's farmhouse again. And everything was right, so right. No more secrets, no more danger, standing between them.

Just two hearts, reaching out, and his that had been for so long locked up, free. Hers, free now, too.

"This is amazing," he said, awed by the beauty of her, how her eyes glowed as she turned from shutting the door. Blue twilight framed her from the windows overlooking the front of the farm. Snow fell gently, fairyland-like, behind her through the trees. Not a storm, not this time. Snow falling like in a dream.

But it was real, all real. He'd somehow stolen back six months of his life. Six months he got to relive.

With Calla.

She shook out of her jacket, tore off her gloves. Helped him with his coat that was just draped over his shoulders, his body still too sore to endure the effort of putting them into coatsleeves.

Six months of extra time might have made him patient, but he didn't feel patient at all.

"I think you're supposed to go straight to bed," she said.

"Hmm. I like the sound of that," he murmured.

"I think you're supposed to behave," she said, laughing.

"Making love with you is behaving," he said. "It's the best kind of behaving."

"I love making love with you," she said, her eyes bold and sweet on his.

"I know. Isn't that great?"

She smiled, hugely, nodded. He loved seeing her happiness, loved seeing how *he* made her happy. Loved seeing how she had changed, accepted herself, believed in herself. That he'd been part of that change blew his mind.

She'd changed his life, too.

He brought her hand to his mouth, kissed her palm. Felt the heat inside building, and knowing she felt the same. But oh, she was trying to be so careful with him.

"I don't want to just live with you here, Calla," he said softly. "I want to marry you."

Her expression froze. "What?" she breathed.

"Marry you. I want you to be mine forever." Forever. He liked that word.

"People will say we haven't known each other long enough."

"People don't know what we know."

Nobody knew about how he'd come back in time. Nobody but him and Calla. It would be too hard to explain. The rumors in Haven about the paranormal aftereffects of the earthquake were dismissed by most.

Not Dane and Calla. They knew the truth, about the earthquake, and about each other.

He put his mouth to her mouth, soft, coaxing, pulled her close where he could feel her heart thumping as hotly as his own. She reached up, sank her fingers into his hair, breathed his name against his lips.

"You're hurt," she said.

"I'm just fine," he said, taking her hand, pulling her back to the bedroom, her bedroom, where he'd spent that first night after she'd found him, and where they'd first made love.

Piece by piece, she helped him, and he helped her, and articles of clothing fell to the floor in the darkened room. There was a time when it would have frightened him how badly he needed her. There was a time it would have frightened her.

Time had a way of changing everything....

"I love you," he told her again.

She smiled. Just smiled. Tears glowed in her eyes. "I love you, too."

"This is the best," he said when he'd laid her on the bed and she'd climbed on top of him so he wouldn't have to support his weight. And now, right there, the two of them connected in the most intimate way possible—that was the best.

He teased his tongue over her heated flesh as she moved over him, capturing her mouth again with his. They built a delicious, hazy friction between them, slow and gentle and in no hurry. They didn't just have an extra six months. They had all the time in the world.

"And it's just," he breathed against her lips, "going to get better. And better and better."

And indeed it did.

* * * * *

Melita had been expecting a chaste quick kiss of the generic variety. But this kiss with Sully was the kind that sparked a dying flame to life. The kind of kiss you can't plan for. The kind of kiss memories are built on.

The memory of her murdered lover, Nemo, came to her then and she made a starved little noise in the back of her throat. She raised her arms and threaded her fingers through Sully's hair, pulled him closer. Felt his body settle, then melt into her.

In that instant her hunger for him grew, and his

for her. She pressed herself to him with more urgency, and he responded in kind.

Melita came out of her kiss-induced memory of Nemo with a start. "Wait a minute." She pushed Sully away from her. "You bastard!"

She spit two nasty words at him in Greek, then wiped his kiss from her lips.

"I thought you deserved some solid proof that I'm still in one piece." He started for the door. "The clock's ticking, honey. Come on, let's get out of here."

"That's it? You sucker me into kissing you, and that's all you have to say?"

"I'm sorry. How's that?"

He didn't sound sorry in the least. "You're—"

"Getting out of this godforsaken prison cell. Stop whining and let's go."

"Not if I was being shot at sunrise. Go. You deserve whatever you get if you walk out that door."

He turned back. "Freedom is what I'm going to get."

"A second of freedom before the guards in the hall shoot you." She jammed her hands on her hips. "And to think I was worried about you."

"If you're staying behind, it's no skin off my ass."

"Wait! What about our deal?"

"You just said you're not coming. Make up your mind."

"Have you forgotten we need a boat?"

"How could I? You keep harping on it."

"I'm not going without a boat. And those guards out there aren't going to just let you walk out of here. You need me and we need a plan."

"I already have a plan. I'm getting out of here. That's the plan."

"I should have realized that you never intended to take me with you from the very beginning. You're a liar and a coward."

Of everything she had read, there was nothing in Sully Paxton's file that hinted he was a coward, but it was the one word that seemed to register in that one-track mind of his. The look he nailed her with a second later was pure venom.

He came at her so quickly she didn't have time to get out of his way. "You know I'm not a coward."

"Prove it. Give me until dawn. I need one more night to put everything in place before we leave the island."

"You're asking me to stay in this cell one more night...and trust you?"

"Yes."

He snorted. "Yesterday you knew they were planning to harm me, but instead of doing something about it you went to bed and never gave me a second thought. Suppose tonight you do the same. By tomorrow I might damn well be in my grave."

"Okay, I screwed up. I won't do it again." Melita sucked in a ragged breath. "I can't leave this minute. Dawn, Sully. Wait until dawn." When he looked as if he was about to say no, she pleaded, "Please wait for me."

"You're asking a lot. The door's open now. I would be a fool to hang around here and trust that you'll be back."

"What you can trust is that I want off this island as badly as you do, and you're my only hope."

"I must be crazy."

"Is that a yes?"

"Dammit!" He turned his back on her. Swore twice more.

"You won't be sorry."

He turned around. "I already am. How about we seal this new deal?"

He was staring at her lips. Suddenly Melita knew what he expected. "We already sealed it."

"One more. You enjoyed it. Admit it."

"I enjoyed it because I was kissing someone else."

He laughed. "That's a good one."

"It's true. It might have been your lips, but it wasn't you I was kissing."

"If that's your excuse for wanting to kiss me, then—"

"I was kissing Nemo."

"What's a nemo?"

Melita gave Sully a look that clearly told him that he was trespassing on sacred ground. She was about to enforce it with a warning when a voice in the hall jerked them both to attention.

She bolted away from the wall. "Get back in bed. Hurry. I'll be here before dawn."

She didn't reach the door before he snagged her arm, pulled her up against him and planted a kiss on her lips that took her completely by surprise.

When he released her, he said, "If you're confused about who just kissed you, the name's Sully. I'll be here waiting at dawn. Don't be late."

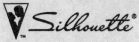

Romantic
SUSPENSE

**Sparked by Danger,
Fueled by Passion.**

Onyxx agent Sully Paxton's only chance of
survival lies in the hands of his enemy's daughter
Melita Krizova. He doesn't know he's a pawn in the
beautiful island girl's own plan for escape. Can
they survive their ruses and their fiery attraction?

*Look for the next installment in the
Spy Games miniseries,*

Sleeping with Danger

by Wendy Rosnau

Available November 2007 wherever you buy books.

ATHENA FORCE

Heart-pounding romance and thrilling adventure.

History repeats itself...unless she can stop it.

Investigative reporter Winter Archer is thrown into writing
a biography of Athena Academy's founder. But someone
out there will stop at nothing—not even murder—to
ensure that long-buried secrets remain hidden.

ATHENA FORCE

Will the women of Athena unravel Arachne's powerful
web of blackmail and death...or succumb to their
enemies' deadly secrets?

Look for

VENDETTA

by *Meredith Fletcher*

*Available November
wherever you buy books.*

REQUEST YOUR FREE BOOKS!

2 FREE NOVELS PLUS 2 FREE GIFTS!

Silhouette® Romantic

SUSPENSE

Sparked by Danger, Fueled by Passion!

YES! Please send me 2 FREE Silhouette® Romantic Suspense novels and my 2 FREE gifts. After receiving them, if I don't wish to receive any more books, I can return the shipping statement marked "cancel." If I don't cancel, I will receive 4 brand-new novels every month and be billed just $4.24 per book in the U.S., or $4.99 per book in Canada, plus 25¢ shipping and handling per book plus applicable taxes, if any*. That's a savings of at least 15% off the cover price! I understand that accepting the 2 free books and gifts places me under no obligation to buy anything. I can always return a shipment and cancel at any time. Even if I never buy another book from Silhouette, the two free books and gifts are mine to keep forever.

240 SDN EEX6   340 SDN EEYJ

Name	(PLEASE PRINT)

Address	Apt. #

City	State/Prov.	Zip/Postal Code

Signature (if under 18, a parent or guardian must sign)

Mail to the Silhouette Reader Service™:
IN U.S.A.: P.O. Box 1867, Buffalo, NY 14240-1867
IN CANADA: P.O. Box 609, Fort Erie, Ontario L2A 5X3

Not valid to current Silhouette Intimate Moments subscribers.

Want to try two free books from another line?
Call 1-800-873-8635 or visit www.morefreebooks.com.

* Terms and prices subject to change without notice. NY residents add applicable sales tax. Canadian residents will be charged applicable provincial taxes and GST. This offer is limited to one order per household. All orders subject to approval. Credit or debit balances in a customer's account(s) may be offset by any other outstanding balance owed by or to the customer. Please allow 4 to 6 weeks for delivery.

Your Privacy: Silhouette is committed to protecting your privacy. Our Privacy Policy is available online at www.eHarlequin.com or upon request from the Reader Service. From time to time we make our lists of customers available to reputable firms who may have a product or service of interest to you. If you would prefer we not share your name and address, please check here. ☐

SRS07

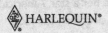

HRIBC03985

Silhouette®
Romantic
SUSPENSE

COMING NEXT MONTH

**#1487 HOLIDAY HEROES—"The Best Noel" by Rachel Lee,
"Christmas at His Command" by Catherine Mann**
Jump into the holiday season with two military-themed short stories
by *New York Times* bestselling author Rachel Lee and RITA® Award-
winning author Catherine Mann.

#1488 KISS OR KILL—Lyn Stone
Mission: Impassioned
When undercover agent Renee Leblanc recognizes Lazlo operative
Mark Alexander at a secret meeting, she fears her alias will be blown.
Mark realizes Renee is following the same lead and proposes they
partner up...but their passion for one another could be deadly.

#1489 SLEEPING WITH DANGER—Wendy Rosnau
Spy Games
Onyxx agent Sully Paxton's only chance of survival lies in the hands of
his enemy's daughter, Melita Krizova. He doesn't know he's a pawn in
the beautiful island girl's own plan for escape. Can they survive each
other's ruses and their fiery attraction?

#1490 SEDUCING THE MERCENARY—Loreth Anne White
Shadow Soldiers
To the rest of the world, Jean-Charles Laroque is a dangerous tyrant.
But Dr. Emily Carlin gains access to his true identity and in doing
so becomes a captive in his game of deception and betrayal—all the
while falling under the mercenary's seductive spell.